So, you're probably wonde
anyway? Well, my name is
right, Fagg. F-A-G-G. *Fagg*. And yes, I have heard
them all before. Faggot, Faggatron, Faggmeister
and my personal favourite – Faggalicious. Have
you finished coming up with your own? Okay,
great, let's continue ...

I'm nineteen years old and I wasted a year of
my life resitting my A-levels, as I considered
them to be of unbelievable importance, when I
could have been travelling the world on a gap
year. However, the truth is that life isn't about
what you know – it's about *who* you know.
Anyway, enough clichés. Truthfully, resitting my
A-levels was the best thing that happened to
me (whoops, there's another) as not only did it
introduce me to the subject of law, but it also
allowed me to move back a year and meet
people I now consider my best friends.

It was after studying law at A-level and
generally mucking about in sixth form that I
decided that I enjoyed it enough to give it a go
at university. The university I chose?
Southampton? No, those gits rejected my
application. So it was a London university I
ended up attending and what a brilliant
experience that was. Great university, great
people, and a completely different way of living

to what I'd experienced in my little village in Surrey.

Before leaving for university I was very much a "stay as close to home as possible" kind of guy. I didn't really like being out of my comfort zone, so much so that even when on holiday with my family I would always think about how easy it was back at home knowing where everything was and knowing most of the people around me. Little things like popping down the shops to get an ice cream would be second nature to me in our little village, but when it came to elsewhere I would become nervous – university certainly changed that.

So, here's my journey …

Chapter 1:

Like I'm sure it was for many of you reading this, the day I left for university was an emotional one. My mum and dad both cried, as did I. I'm also sure that, like me, many of you reading this had two days to choose from when moving into your university halls. Well, like the keen bean I was, I headed up on the first day expecting everyone to do the same. Well, that was a mistake.

I arrived at 08:00 on the dot.

Even the people running enrolment were amazed at my eagerness as I walked into my halls carrying far more than I actually needed.

That's the amazing thing when moving to uni – or anywhere, in fact – you look at stuff that you haven't batted an eyelid at for years and then all of a sudden you're like, "oh, there's that African drum I beat the crap out of for half a day, I'll take that with me!" So, as I lugged my African bongos along the corridor, it suddenly sunk in that I wasn't just the only person in my flat but in fact my entire halls (which only held a modest two hundred people).

With the flat to myself, I set about putting away the numerous items I had brought with me with my mum. Frying pans, plates, cutlery and even a blender – because somehow I had convinced myself university was where I was going to become healthy. I'd dreamt up this idea of me sipping on kale and avocado smoothies with the body of a god, like some fitness model on Instagram. In reality, I think we all know university is actually where people eat an extortionate amount of takeaways and drink too much, so the blender was about as pointless as a glass door on a toilet.

After unpacking everything, I said my goodbyes to my mum as quickly as possible. Like all teenagers, I didn't want to be seen in the same room as one of their "uncool" parents, let alone showing them love or affection! And so as my mum closed my bedroom door behind her and headed back to the car, my uni life and newfound independence officially began.

It was a short four hours later, when I was still sat in my room with no Wi-Fi or TV, that I realised I wished my mum had stayed around for a bit longer (say another three and a half hours or something). It's a lot more boring and sad to sit in a room by yourself than it is to sit talking to one of your parents ...

Eventually, though, people began to arrive in my halls, however the bad news was there was still no sign of anyone actually moving into my flat.

Then, suddenly, I heard movement down the corridor.

The front door opened and then footsteps drew closer. I listened carefully as whoever it was walked past my door and into a room just up from mine. Well, after all that waiting I wanted to get out there and say hello, but instead I found myself stalling, unable to gather up the courage to open my door. I paced back and forth, overthinking my opening line like a comedian about to start his stand-up show. I rehearsed my handshake and "hey, how's it going?" in my bedroom mirror.

Then there was a knock at my door. I froze.

"Hello? Is someone in there?" a voice asked.

"Hey," I replied.

"I'm Freddie, I've just moved into the flat," the voice continued.

"Oh nice, me too."

Then silence.

"So, you gonna open the door or are we going to keep pretending we're on blind date?"

I opened the door to see Freddie, a young, broad-shouldered man stood in front of me. He was just a little shorter than my five foot ten inches, but much more built and far more tanned. His dark, matching black jeans and t-shirt contrasted the warm white smile on his face. Staring back at him, there was me – a pasty white guy with out of control curly blonde hair and blue eyes with hardly an ounce of fat on him. As close to a bean pole as possible, really.

He held out a big, inviting hand. "How you doing, man?" he asked.

"Yeah, good thanks, mate, my name's Luke," I said, squeezing his hand slightly, trying to show some masculinity.

"You been here long?" he asked.

"No," I lied. "Only about thirty minutes," I lied again.

"That's good, you would be bored any longer without any Wi-Fi," Freddie said, gesturing at a small white box on the wall behind him.

I have to admit this was only the second time in my life I had seen a broadband router. Our broadband at home was essentially not ours. To be exact, it was our neighbours. They very kindly gave us their password so we could use it through the connecting wall between our terraced houses. Yep, that's the truth, and to make matters worse that had only just happened! It was brand new technology to me and my family. Before then, while the rest of the world had moved on to wireless broadband, we were still using dial up internet up until the end of 2016!

Each day, the same thing would happen.

"Nobody on the phone for the next couple of hours, just downloading the e-mails!" Dad would shout. Then that incredible dial up tone would start. Da da da da da da da diiiidoooo da dim dum duh dum ... and then you would sit for two agonising hours to download a single e-mail. And if there was anything attached to that e-mail, well, you might as well forget about contacting anyone via the house phone for the rest of the week! It would be painstakingly slow to sit there as a picture of a flower Aunty Christine had sent you from her time at the Chelsea Flower Show loaded pixel by pixel.

"Shall we grab a beer anyway?" Freddie asked.

I glanced at the clock on the bedroom wall. It read 14:00. I had never really drunk alcohol heavily before 18:00, but trying to seem like the cool dude I wasn't, I accepted his invitation to try to earn some street cred and made my way along the purple carpeted corridor down to the kitchen.

The kitchen was large and open plan, which seemed to be the same for virtually every university I had visited on open days. There were two ovens and two sets of hobs with numerous cupboards to store things in positioned around one half of the room. Some cupboards had locks on with accompanying keys, ready to be used by anyone who thought their new flatmates might be after their food. There was a large kitchen worktop in the middle of the room where you could prepare food or, in our case, lay out the beer we were going to consume. As you can imagine, being students, the beer was the cheapest, most horrible tasting beer there was.

The rest of the kitchen accommodated a large wooden table with six green plastic chairs circled around it. They were horrible and flimsy and I couldn't find a comfortable position in them no matter how much I twisted and turned. Overall, though, the kitchen was well above the standards I had seen in other universities and was very spacious considering there was only five of us in the flat.

Freddie picked up two bottles and brought them over to the table. He sat down opposite me and slid one across the smooth, wooden surface towards me. I snatched it off the table as it glided towards me and held it aloft in front of me, inviting him to cheers.

He smirked and we chinked bottles.

"To the first of many." He smiled.

The clock struck 17:00 and I looked at the empty crates of lager in front of me. Well, I say crates – there was actually only one but I was so drunk I was seeing double. Breathing deeply and slowly, I tried to regain some function and control over my body.

"I'll get another crate," said Freddie, getting up from his seat.

"You what?" I slurred. I had not drunk so much in such a short amount of time before and I dared not move because I knew any attempt to walk would result in a fall.

In contrast, Freddie had no such problems. Like a professional from Strictly Come Dancing, he floated across the kitchen floor with not so much as a hint of trouble. He approached the kitchen door, but it opened before he could grab a hold of the handle.

There, stood in the doorway, were two girls. Both with beautiful long hair. One blonde, one brunette.

"Hi," they both said at the same time.

"I'm Layla," said the blonde.

"And I'm Anahita, but you can call me Anna," said the brunette.

Anna was slightly shorter than Layla but both had the same big smile and brought a certain warmth to the room only certain people are capable of.

Freddie introduced himself, no slip of the tongue, just fluent and stylish.

Now, they say first impressions count and Freddie had just passed with flying colours. If he were a diver, he had just performed a triple somersault with a half twist and pike and been awarded straight tens.

Then it was my turn. A belly flop may have been a good analogy.

"Hshiii." I dribbled.

Both Layla and Anna's eyes widened in horror at the noise they just heard.

"Errrmmm, hi," they replied.

They looked over at the kitchen counter and spotted the crate of beer and put two and two together.

"Someone has quickly embraced the uni life," laughed Anna.

Freddie invited them to join us, gesturing at the free chairs around the table. The girls looked at each and smiled before running off to their rooms to find a bottle of wine.

And so, new and long friendships began to form.

Chapter 2:

I sat in the kitchen still feeling slightly worse for wear, but better after being given water by Layla. She and Anna had fetched their bottles of wine and by the sound of it they tasted as bad as our beer. While fetching their alcohol, they had also come across the last member of our flat, Frank.

He was a long-haired fella with a rocky and edgy look about him. He had wristbands with the names of different bands on (none of which I recognised) and heavy-looking shoes with a metal chain hanging from his jeans. He had said very little so far and was sat twiddling away making roll up cigarettes, which, by the look of them, contained a little bit more than just tobacco.

"So, I think I have a fun way of us getting to know each other a bit better," said Layla. "Let's go around the circle and we each say something unique about ourselves."

Well, it turned out Anna was half Iranian and Freddie used to be a very good amateur boxer – winning twenty-three out of twenty-four fights. Frank was next and he took us all by surprise as he boldly stated the he could run through walls ... Yep, he genuinely said that.

"Run through walls?" I questioned, thinking I must have misheard him.

"Yeah, mate, I can do it no problem."

Well, being as intoxicated as we were, and Frank being as confident as he was, we decided that we all had to see this. Having no concern for Frank's health or safety at the time, we got everyone out into the corridor and told Frank to run at the wall at the far end as hard as he could before bursting through it like The Hulk on a rampage.

The funny thing was that Frank had made his wall bashing claim with such authority I genuinely believed him. With our backs against the walls of the corridor we watched as he got down in the starting position of a sprinter. The anticipation grew as in silence, Frank looked up at his target and then set off down the hallway, pumping his legs hard against the ground. The noise of his heavy boots hitting the floor resonated through the walls as he picked up speed. Ten metres from the end I felt my fist clench in expectancy.

Three, two, one … Bang!

The noise made as Frank hit the wall was horrendous, like a paving slab being dropped onto concrete below.

Layla grabbed my hand at the fright of it all before letting it go in embarrassment when she realised what she had done.

For all of half a second, I actually thought he had made it through. However, he hadn't. Instead, he was lying on his back, totally motionless.

"Frank?" I said worriedly.

The rest of us looked at each other with genuine concern across our faces. Then, like a zombie out of a horror movie, Frank dragged himself off the floor.

"That was awesome!" he yelled, stumbling about, holding his arms in the air.

There was a brief silence before we all started celebrating. "Yeah!" we all shouted together.

Then, without warning, Frank pushed himself off the wall that he had just knocked himself out on and started off again, this time heading for the front door behind us.

"Move!" he shouted.

We parted like the red sea, hugging the wall like geckos desperate to avoid getting in the way.

He hurtled past us in a flash of black before bouncing off the heavy fire door and flying back about two metres, before again lying totally motionless. This time, though, he didn't get up.

"Frank?" I asked again. "Are you okay?"

"Maybe we should check his pulse," said Freddie. He leaned down and pressed two fingers against his neck. "There's a heartbeat."

We all let out a sigh of relief.

I leant down to make sure he was breathing too. A whiff of cigarettes from his mouth confirmed he was.

"Well, I guess we just wait for him to come 'round," Freddie said with a shrug.

We all stood, biting our fingernails for what felt like an eternity before Frank eventually opened his eyes.

"Awww, my head," he moaned as he came to his senses. He sat up, cupped his head in his hands and rocked back and forth on his backside.

We all told him to take it easy given what had just happened and the beating his body had taken. Thankfully, he took the words on board and sat for a few minutes with a pack of frozen peas on his head to ease the pain. After about five minutes and claiming to feel a lot better, he put his arms down by his sides and shook his head from side to side frantically before stopping and opening his eyes widely.

"I need a spliff after that," he moaned, and before we could say anything he rose to his feet and made his way out of the flat door with a joint on its way to his lips, as if nothing had happened.

"Well, that kid is nuts," laughed Freddie.

"I have never seen anything like that in my entire life," laughed Layla.

I was in hysterics. I just couldn't stop laughing. I stumbled into the kitchen, hardly able to catch my breath after what I had just witnessed. It became infectious as the others began to lose it as well. We had known this guy less than thirty minutes but could already tell he was going to be a loose cannon for the rest of the year.

After exhausting our bodies of energy from the endless amount of giggles, we managed to sit down and talk about what we could do on our first night at uni. Staying in and drinking was a suggestion made but on such a high from the Frank party piece, as it was now known, we thought we needed to head out.

So, it wasn't long before we were chugging the last of our drinks down and heading out the front door together. On the stairwell of the halls, we got the sense that we weren't the only ones enjoying ourselves that night. The smell of alcohol was strong in the hallway and we could hear music blaring from flats as we made our way down the long, twisting staircase.

Opening the front door to the building, the fresh air hit us. It was a cold, crisp night and despite the alcohol warming my body, I was soon regretting my choice of a short-sleeved t-shirt. We followed the road in front of our building around a long right hand turn before arriving at a bus stop. It was heaving with people. Many were drinking and there was a lot of singing and chanting going on. It reminded me more of football fans travelling to a game than a university.

We shuffled our way along the pavement and huddled with the other people, like a group of penguins seeking some warmth and protection from the cold.

"This is cosy," laughed Anna.

I looked around and took in my surroundings. I felt tiny amongst everyone. All the guys seemed to be six-foot-tall and built like rhinos and then there was me – a lot shorter and built like a stick insect.

Suddenly, there was a shout of "bus!" behind us and everyone turned to see a purple, bendy bus weaving its way around the corner and towards us all. People began to shuffle forward and it wasn't long before people were pushed off the curb and into the road.

The bus driver must have seen this happen a thousand times before and stopped dead in his tracks about twenty-five metres up from us all. All two-hundred-odd of us stared at him, wondering what he was doing. He then flashed his lights and we saw the doors slide open. There was no hesitation – it was every man for himself.

Layla grabbed my arm and we ran together with Anna and Freddie close behind.

"Go for the back doors!" shouted Freddie. "Everyone will aim for the front, run past them."

We followed his instructions and, arriving at the back doors, swung ourselves inside. Despite being as quick as we were, there were no seats left but we found a pole to cling on to and managed to keep a space free for Freddie and Anna who jumped in not long after us.

Although we were on board, we still had problems. This bus was not built to hold two hundred people, at a push, it could possibly stretch to one hundred and fifty, but that was not going to stop the angry mob behind us having a go. The limited amount of room we had around us soon disappeared.

Layla and I were now crammed into a corner with Anna and Freddie pressing us in.

"Usually, I would ask for someone's number before getting this close," I joked with Layla.

She laughed and jabbed me in the ribs with her finger, using the little room she had left to do so.

People continued to cram themselves on before eventually the last few gave up and accepted their fate of waiting until the next one came along. The doors squeezed shut and the heavy bus made a grinding start on its way to the student union.

Thankfully, it was a short bus ride, but we all arrived a little drained having been crammed in like sardines. We hopped off and joined the long, snaking queue leading to the cashier at the entrance to the student union. We shuffled our way along, chatting to people in the queue as we slowly made our way to the front. It was

£5 entry and as we passed the bouncers, we could feel the bass of the music pulsating through our bodies.

We took a short walk to a set of double doors and opened them and were immediately hit by the force of noise coming from behind them.

In front of us was an enormous room. A long bar to the right hand side was packed with people and being manned by staff who were running around frantically trying to keep up with the drunken orders flying at them. To the left of us were a couple of small steps leading down to a huge dancefloor, which was winged by another two bars. In front of the dancefloor was a stage filled with multi-coloured lights and smoke with a DJ positioned directly in the middle, throwing his hands in the air to the beat of the music.

The place was absolutely rocking with the crowd jumping up and down to the rhythm of the music.

Freddie rounded us up and pointed towards one of the bars that was less busy than the other two. We followed him single file, holding one another's hands to make sure we didn't lose each other in the chaos around us.

A quick round of jägerbombs and we were ready for the dance floor. We weaved our way through the crowd before finding an area we could all gather together.

I have never been much of a dancer and this was quickly evident to the others as I struggled to bring any sort of rhythm to my body. It was as if my arms and legs were controlled by two different brains and they couldn't function together. One second, my arms were flying around like Louis Spence, with absolutely no movement from my legs, and the next second there was the complete reverse, with my legs producing some kind of Kankan motion while my arms were fixed by my sides as if they'd been superglued. In contrast, the others were great at dancing and as a result I felt well out of my depth.

In an attempt to win some respect from my new flatmates, I looked around for some extra room so I could pull off a couple of more complicated moves. I spotted a gap opening up ahead of me and flung myself forward into it.

Unfortunately, I could not have timed my jump any worse.

Just as my feet left the floor, a guy stepped out into the space, holding four drinks in his hands.

There was nothing I could do.

I yelled and stuck out my arms to act as a cushion, but the whole weight of my body followed and I smashed into him, sending his drinks flying.

I looked up from the puddle of drink on the floor to see his face covered in coke and his white t-shirt wet with the brown mixture. I immediately offered my apologies and asked whether I could buy him a new drink and get him napkins. However, I could see from the anger in his eyes and the throbbing vein appearing in his forehead that the offer would not be accepted and he wanted something else – revenge.

People around us had seen the commotion and backed off, forming a circle around us – much like a mini boxing ring. Looking around the human wall that now surrounded us and then back to the wet gentleman in front of me, I suddenly gauged just how big he was. I began to open my mouth to offer another apology but before I could get a word out, the giant of a man swung a muscular right arm round and smashed his fist into the side of my face.

Pain shot threw my cheekbone, but somehow I stayed on my feet. Like a baby taking its first steps, I struggled to keep my balance. Staggering from side to side, I expected another hit to come raining down, but as I looked up through my blurred vision, I saw a figure lunge forward and catch my attacker with a punch of their own.

It was Freddie. Without hesitation he had stepped forward and delivered his own hit right on this guy's nose. The big lad toppled down as if in slow motion and hit the floor.

Still dazed and not thinking straight, I didn't move as I tried to make sense of what was happening.

Suddenly, an arm grabbed me from behind – it was Layla.

"Let's go!" she shouted. She pulled my arm behind her as I wobbled through the crowd, just about able to keep my footing as we picked up pace.

In a flash, we were at the exit and running across to the bus stop. My face was pulsating. It felt like my head was getting bigger and bigger with every heartbeat – which I could hear pounding away deafeningly in my ears.

Despite the pain, I didn't want to let on just how much agony I was in, trying to hold on to any pride I had left.

"You okay, Luke?" asked Layla.

"Yeah, all good," I lied, trying to smile through the pain.

Outside, stood in the fresh night air, it suddenly dawned on me – what about that hit from Freddie? "Freddie where did you learnt that sort of punch?" I blurted out.

"I used to box, didn't I?" he replied in a calm, smooth voice as if nothing had happened.

"Of course! Well that explains that then … fuck me, though, he was massive and you knocked him down like he was a child" I said.

Freddie laughed.

I sat down at the bus stop on the cold metal ledge that bus companies somehow consider a "seat" before leaning my head back against the glass of the bus shelter and shutting my eyes. I pressed my tongue against the inside of my cheek, where most of the pain was coming from, and instantly regretted it. I leant forward with the pain and opened my eyes.

Anna noticed my reaction. "You don't have to act brave," she whispered to me. "I was impressed you managed to stay on your feet, to be honest."

"Thanks," I whispered back, making sure the others couldn't hear.

I looked up and saw the bus coming up the road towards us. I gathered myself together and got to my feet, still feeling groggy. I looked around one last time before getting on to make sure there was no sign of my attacker – the last thing I wanted was to be on the same bus with him heading back to campus.

With the coast clear, I hopped on board and sat down with the others on the horrendously smelly seats. That's the thing with buses, the multi-coloured seats aren't so much for aesthetical reasons but more to cover up the endless amount of drink and food people have had fall out of their mouths or hands and then rubbed into the fabric.

Trying to ignore the mess made by the last passengers, we continued to share things about ourselves. Turns out Layla had a friend who'd had sex on a plane! I hadn't even had sex full stop.

Oh, yeah, forgot to mention that …

We arrived home to our halls to find Frank stood outside with a couple of smokers. Isn't it amazing how weed smokers just naturally find each other? It's like they have some kind of weed radar built into their bodies. Well, Frank and his new friends were all high as a kite and Frank was holding something pink and plastic in his hands.

"What the hell is that?" I asked him.

"It's a plastic flamingo," he replied as if it was nothing out the ordinary.

"What are you doing with it?" Layla asked before I could.

"I was walking back from the bar and saw a woman had two in her front garden so I decided to pinch one for my room," he replied.

It was at this point that I realised it wasn't even worth asking Frank these sort of questions anymore because he was so far into a world of his own that this sort of behaviour was just standard to him.

We made our way into the flat with Frank following behind us and gathered in the kitchen where we all sat down and continued talking.

It was amazing – despite only just meeting these guys, I felt I could talk about anything to them. It was so easy going and the conversations took my mind off the ever-growing lump on the side of my face, which now had the same bag of frozen peas Frank had used strapped to it, with the help of a tea towel.

I looked pathetic, quite frankly, but I just didn't care, I knew these guys weren't going to judge me. We stayed up till about 05:00 until eventually we all had to call it a day and head to bed just as the sun began to rise for my second day at uni.

The next morning, (well, I say morning – I woke up at 15:00) my head was thumping. I forced myself to get out of bed and make my way to my en suite, which only cost me an extra £150 a month to have (and yes, I am being sarcastic). I looked in the mirror and it's hard to describe what I saw, but imagine a guy with half a purple tennis ball sticking out of his cheek. I mean, as looks go, this was up there with the worst. I looked like a prisoner who had just been beaten up after snitching on his gang.

I showered and got changed before making my way to the kitchen. Anna and Freddie were both cooking and let out a cheer as I entered.

"How you doing, Tyson?" Freddie laughed.

I laughed back and instantly bemoaned myself as pain shot through my jaw.

I sat down and Anna brought me over a cup of coffee. This was another new experience for me as I had only ever drunk tea. Not once in nineteen years had I had a cup of coffee, which is a bit mad, looking back on it.

This must have transpired in my facial expression as, without me saying anything, Anna just looked at me and said, "To make it through uni, you are going to have to learn to drink coffee."

I took a sip and, despite hating the taste, I forced it down my parched mouth.

Freddie and Anna joined me at the table, shortly followed by Layla who had also only just woken up.

"Any plans for today?" Layla asked us.

"Chilling," replied Freddie. "Although I might go thing."

"What's 'thing'?" I asked.

"You know, *thing*."

"No, what's that?"

"You know, 'thing', where all the things happen."

"Was it just me who took a bang to the head last night?" I asked, perplexed as to what I was hearing.

"The SU."

"Why didn't you just say SU?"

"It's 'thing', innit?"

"No, it's the SU, not 'thing'."

"But 'thing' is shorter."

"Well, I'm lost. So you mean you might go to the SU?"

"Yeah, I might go for the football."

"Right ... Okay, we'll go 'thing' for the football."

"See, you're getting it!" laughed Freddie.

"It's the last day before lectures anyway, so it would be nice just to have a session but not get too carried away."

Chapter 3:

About six hours later, I stumbled out of the SU with Anna, Layla and Freddie. I was whirling my t-shirt around my head. Arsenal FC had won. I didn't even support Arsenal! But it seemed everyone at this uni did, so why not join them and have a good time?

Freddie had his shirt off as well. He put an arm over my shoulder and yelled, "What do we think of Tottenham?"

Along with the forty people walking alongside us, I shouted, "Shit!"

"What do we think of shit?"

"Tottenham!" We jumped up and down and carried on singing songs all the way back to the flat, enjoying every moment and completely forgetting about the lectures we had coming up tomorrow morning.

The game had been a late kick off, but with the victory encouraging more drinks after it finished, we ended up at the flat at about 21:00. Again, upon arriving back we found Frank outside having a cigarette and clutching a pink flamingo.

"You love that thing, don't you?" I laughed.

"It's actually a new one," said Frank. "She replaced the one I borrowed with another."

"You are one hell of a weird human being," I laughed.

"Thanks." Frank smiled.

We left Frank and his new pet toy and stumbled upstairs to our flat. Feeling as intoxicated as we were, we should've said, like any normal person, *okay, let's hit the hay and get a good night's sleep for tomorrow*. Well, intoxicated Luke isn't that sensible so instead I thought it best we went out.

Amazingly, the others didn't even need that much persuasion. In fact, they actually thought it was a great idea rather than a terrible one. We all went off to our rooms to get changed and even rallied up Frank, who, amazingly, in the short time we had left him for, had got high. I actually couldn't believe this guy could still function considering just how much he smoked.

We headed out (bearing in mind this was a Sunday) to the SU nightclub. God knows why it was open, but it was. We paid entry and followed the bass of the music just like the night before. We entered the main room and, in doing so, doubled the number of people there. There was us five, one DJ and four bar staff.

"Maybe everyone has forgotten the bit where they jump out and shout surprise," I said.

There was literally nobody there.

Now, if this wasn't a sign that really I should be in bed, then I don't know what was.

But, nope, before I knew it I was at the bar and saying those dreaded words: "Jägerbombs, please."

We literally had our own private disco. We requested song after song and with another ten people joining after having the same stupid idea as us, I had one of the weirdest but most fun nights of my life.

I don't know how I got home that night, all I do remember is waking the next morning to the sound of my alarm. I thumped it quiet and glanced at the time. I thought I was still drunk because my clock read 08:50, which meant I had ten minutes until my first lecture of the year.

"Shit!" I shouted in sudden realisation at my mistake. I bolted out of bed completely naked, scrambling for something to wear. In my haste, I threw on the same outfit I wore last night and ran out the door, with the fumes of alcohol still emitting from my clothes and body.

It turns out it takes exactly ten minutes to run from my flat to the law building where my lectures were being held. I arrived bang on 09:00, pumping sweat (which was probably fifty per cent alcohol), where I was greeted by a lovely gentleman at the door of the lecture hall. He was in his forties and was the epitome of dapper. Shirt, jacket, glasses and perfectly sculpted slicked back hair.

"You must be Luke," he said, reaching out and offering his right hand with the left holding a clipboard and pen.

"That's me," I said as I gasped for air.

"Come on in, all the others are already in there and we are about to get started."

I walked in and everyone turned to look at me.

Similarly to meeting Anna and Layla, my first impression was again not great. I looked like a relative of Quasimodo with a slightly purple lump on my face and a hunched back that I had formed in order to help me avoid throwing up. I then also realised I was wearing a white t-shirt that had a drink stain down the front from the previous night.

eard sniggering and could feel myself turning red as I walked over to the only empty seat left at the back of the room where I sat down.

"Right then, everyone. My name is Charles and I will be your lecturer for law this year. We will be covering a number of different modules so I suggest you get out a pen and make a note of them so you know what books to purchase."

Well, in my haste to leave my room, not only had I picked up a t-shirt most tramps would throw away, but I had also forgotten a pen and paper. I turned to the person next to me, who had their back to me and was fumbling in their bag.

"Excuse me?" I asked politely. "Do you have a pen and paper I could possibly borrow?"

To my horror, the individual turned and I was faced with a man with a wonky nose and two black eyes. It was the guy who had hit me on my first night out.

"Arghhh!" I blurted out of surprise.

Everyone in the room turned to look at the two of us after the shriek I had let out. We awkwardly stared at one another until the monster of a man pushed a pen and a piece of paper across to me.

"Everything okay over there?" asked Charles.

"All good," I lied, fearing for my life.

My desk mate was still staring at me, looking deep into my soul – possibly thinking about ripping it out.

We sat and listened to Charles go through what the year held for us, but to be honest, I was so worried about being attacked by my desk mate that I didn't take in a lot – I was more concerned about the words that might be said at my funeral.

Eventually, Charles finished and proceeded to ask if anyone wanted to take part in a mock trial. Naturally, nobody volunteered and so he picked two people. Yep, you guessed right, those two people were my new friend and I.

We made our way to the front.

"If you would like to sit there, Andy," Charles said, gesturing at a chair.

Andy – well I guess that will be the name that appears in the newspaper article about my murder, I thought to myself.

"Okay, Luke, what you are going to do is cross examine Andy. It looks as if Andy has quite an injury, as in fact you do, Luke. This could make a good role play. Let's say Andy has been involved in fight and is accused of grievous bodily harm – GBH."

If only Charles knew the whole story, I thought to myself.

I straightened up and tried to compose myself in front of the hundred-odd people in the lecture room.

"So, Andy, run me through the events as you see them on the night of the incident," I said.

"Well, I was having a great night until I had my own drink spilt over me by an intoxicated individual. I then proceeded to push him and I was hit to the ground by one of his friends."

"Well, that's not completely true, is it?" I quizzed before I could stop myself.

"What do you mean?"

"Well, you didn't push the victim, did you? You proceeded to punch them without warning, while they were trying to explain the situation to you."

Andy's face twisted in anger.

"The friend then punched you, acting in self-defence for the victim," I continued.

Andy slammed his fist into the table.

I jumped back and yelped as did three girls in the front row.

"That's not true!" Andy shouted.

Charles began to clap.

I spun round in shock.

"In all my years of working as a lecturer, that is some of the best role play I have seen at this uni from first time mock trialists!" he praised.

I turned back to see Andy still raging, almost frothing at the mouth like a like a guard dog who's just spotted a trespasser. Charles was oblivious to the actual situation — much like everyone else in the lecture hall. It seemed real to everyone else because it *was* real! This bloke was mental — possessed, even. Everyone in the hall was now following Charles' lead and applauding, there was even a "Woop!" thrown in.

I wish I could have savoured the moment and taken in the applause from my fellow peers, but I was too terrified.

With my safety in mind, I scuttled my way back to my chair, grabbing my stuff and heading for the exit before Andy could catch up. I power walked so quickly back to my flat I was nearly running. I constantly checked over my shoulder for a follower, but thankfully there was no sign of one. I arrived back at the flat door where I met Frank.

"How's it going, man?" he mumbled with a cigarette dangling from his mouth.

"Not the best," I replied breathlessly.

I quickly made my way up the stairs to my flat, taking two at a time before bursting into the kitchen where Anna, Layla and Freddie were sat. They immediately saw something was wrong and asked if I was okay, suggesting it looked as if I had seen a ghost.

I felt sick.

I steadied myself and took a seat at the table. The others looked at me, concerned, as I sat and looked straight ahead, my mind ticking over and processing what had just happened.

"Luke?" Layla asked, resting a hand on my shoulder.

I flinched at her touch, still on edge and with adrenaline pumping through my veins. I composed myself and proceeded to explain the events of the morning.

After they had all finished laughing, I asked for their advice.

"Leave uni," was Freddie's suggestion.

How was I going to continue attending lectures with this maniac on the same course as me? I know people tend to skip the odd lecture at university but I couldn't miss the whole year!

"This is terrible," I said, burying my face into my hands. "This has to be a dream ... tell me I'm dreaming!" I pleaded.

We went through a number of ideas.

Killing Andy was one option considered but deemed a little extreme after a short discussion. A disguise for myself was another that was, again, swiftly put aside. Eventually, the most sensible idea – and the one we decided to run with – was to sit as far away from Andy in lectures as possible and leave the premises immediately after to avoid any confrontation. We also Googled stab proof vests but they were quite a lot more expensive than we thought and so it was decided I should just risk death and save the money for alcohol. Priorities.

It came to about 17:00 and I was exhausted. I'd had two hours of lectures all day. *Just* two ... but

I felt like I'd been hit by a truck. I could not believe how mentally drained I was. I asked Anna if she felt the same. She explained that she used to until she discovered day naps. A short forty-minute sleep during the day, usually around lunch or after eating meant she was fully energised for the rest of the day.

Well, hearing this, I had to give it a go. I lost my day nap virginity shortly after the conversation with Anna and after it I felt like a new man.

I headed back to the kitchen with liveliness running through my body. I insisted to the others that we do something that night and Anna laughed at how the nap had clearly worked wonders. We sat down and discussed options like a boardroom meeting from The Apprentice.

Layla explained that she had seen that the hide and seek society was running that night. A hide and seek society? Universities literally had a society for everything, it seemed! A short show of hands later and it was decided that was our event for the night.

I wasn't really sure what I was expecting, but when we arrived at the meeting point – a large lecture hall – I was amazed to find at least fifty people already there. Most were stood in little huddles and I couldn't work out if they were discussing tactics or just getting to know each other.

"Wow!" we all gasped, amazed at the turnout. We made our way to the front where we found a leaflet outlining the society with its aims and rules.

A short while later, a student stepped forward in front of everyone. His name was Mark and he was the head of the hide and seek society. What a title to have! And you could tell how much Mark loved the position he had at the top by the enthusiasm and smile he had spread across his face as he introduced himself to everyone.

He quickly went through the rules on the leaflet but in slightly more detail. In truth, it was quite simple – hide and don't be found. If you were found, you then helped the seeker. You were allowed anywhere in the lecture hall in which we were stood in and also in the library, which was just up the corridor. Layla, Anna, Freddie and I all agreed the library was the best bet, a much bigger area with three floors and a huge amount of hiding places. We were all given t-shirts with "Hider" written on them so we could be differentiated from the "Normal people" in the library.

The seeker for the first game of the year was Paul, a short, podgy fella who wore glasses and the person I was going to do everything in my power to avoid. I was so desperate to win I may have got a little carried away. As Paul turned to face the wall and begin counting to a hundred, I sprinted down the corridor to the library. Rather embarrassingly, my first steps into the library were not to rent a book or do some research but to play a game of hide and seek ...

The library itself was enormous but amazingly quiet. That, however, didn't last long as my heavy footsteps echoed around its walls and I began gasping for air, having put too much effort into getting away as quickly as possible. I could hear a few tuts and murmurs of disapproval at the fact I had been so loud. I turned to see another five people come storming in but none of them were my flatmates. Eventually, Freddie arrived and we both agreed to work together to help find a suitable spot.

We decided the lift would take too long, so headed for the stairs and made our way up, taking two at a time. We crept as carefully as possible but were still making far too much noise and disturbing people who were trying to study. On the first floor, we had a quick scan around at options but there were just endless amounts of computers and no real opportunities to properly hide ourselves away.

We bounded up the stairs to the next level. This floor made for much better options with high bookcases and study desks scattered around the place. The bookcases were about ten feet tall and would make an excellent hiding spot if you could reach the top. Freddie saw the idea I had in my head and ushered me across to one of them. He bent down and cupped his hands for me to place my foot into. As carefully as I could, I held on to the bookcase as I pushed down on his hands with my right foot. I was well short of the top but to my amazement, Freddie kept lifting me higher and higher.

He had his arms at shoulder height and I was only just short of getting a good grip on the top shelf to heave myself up. He whispered up to me and explained that I needed to step on his shoulders so he could readjust his hands. I did so and like some kind of circus act, he stumbled from side to side trying to keep his balance as I clung on to the bookcase. It was very precarious at first but eventually Freddie found his footing.

He held out his hands again but this time they were separated. He nodded up to me to encourage me to stand a foot on either one.

Knowing we were quickly running out of time, I reluctantly obliged. To my amazement, Freddie lifted my ankles above his head – the strength he had was truly incredible. I got hold of the top shelf and swung myself on top of it. It was about the width of my body, which meant nobody below could really see me if I remained still. I peered over the edge to see Freddie give me a thumbs up.

"Cheers, mate," I whispered.

Freddie quickly set off to find his own spot.

Up as high as I was, I felt like a king. I could actually touch the ceiling and was looking down on everyone and everything below me. I shuffled myself forward on the shelf and could see everything on the far side of the floor I was on. There, I could already see Paul in the distance with about five people he had already found and were now helping him. I shuffled myself back to get out of sight just in case there was the small chance they could see me. I then laid myself as flat as possible to make sure as little, if any, of my body was showing.

I continued to lay there for about five minutes thinking how things may have gone for the others hiding. I decided to risk a peek. I slowly pushed my chest off the shelf and like a curious meerkat twisted my head from side to side, scanning the area around me. There was nothing to my right but to the left I could see there was now a whole army with Paul. I ducked down quickly again to avoid being seen. Then, to my horror, I heard voices beneath me. Had they seen me? The voices bickered about where I could be, clearly not having a clue I was right above them.

I plucked up the courage to look over the side where the voices were coming from. My heart was racing! How on earth could a game of hide and seek become so intense? Looking over, I saw two girls chatting and, would you believe it, Freddie was with them!

He looked up at me and mouthed the word, "move."

The seriousness in his eyes suggested to me that there were more people on the way and I needed to get out of there quickly before I was cornered. I peered about to assess my options. The main area of the floor was off limits as it was heaving with seekers, but the corner to my left did not have anyone occupying it and there was another set of stairs. I needed to somehow get over there.

As quietly as possible, I adopted a crouch position. If I could, I needed to hop on to the bookcase that ran parallel to the one I was on. Jumping down from where I was would instantly result in being found as I would make too much noise right next to the two girls. With adrenaline taking over my body, I stretched my right leg out and over to the other bookcase. It was closer than it looked and I confidently pushed my weight off my back foot and sprung myself forward onto it. I smiled to myself at my small accomplishment.

I did the same thing for the next three bookcases and could hear the voices of the girls becoming more distant. The fourth bookcase was slightly further way than the others which proved more of a challenge. I swung my leg across and go the tip of my shoe on to the top shelf. In my haste to keep moving, I pushed off and instantly my leading leg slipped from what little grip it had.

In desperation, I grabbed at anything I could with both hands, praying for something to hold on to.

By sheer luck, I caught on to one of the shelves with my right hand and had just enough grip to stop myself crashing to the floor. I hung helplessly about three feet above the ground. It wasn't that far down and any sensible person would have just let themselves drop.

Stupidly, I thought I could make things easier and lower myself further to the ground. I heaved my right leg up to a shelf above me and then, with a good grip, swung the other leg up level to it. I then made a terrible mistake by pushing my bottom out to adopt a kind of abseiling position.

With my weight pushed away from the bookcase, I heard some creaking. I looked around trying to work out where it was coming from, but once I did it was too late.

I let out a shout as the bookcase I held onto begun to fall with my weight into the adjacent bookcase.

It was a miracle I wasn't crushed.

Instead, I ended up right at the bottom of the two in a sort of tunnel, which was filled with books that had just slid from their shelves. I now didn't want to just avoid being found by the "seekers" but *anyone* in the library.

I scrambled on my hands and knees, pushing the books aside and wriggling my way through the tight gap. The noise created by all of my shenanigans was enormous and I could hear people running over to see what had happened. I managed to just get out of sight in time and bolted down the stairs as quickly as I could. I arrived at the bottom and decided to just take a seat at one of the computers on the ground floor.

It wasn't long until a member of the seeking team found me, but I didn't care. I was just happy that I had managed to escape unnoticed. I even had to pretend that I knew nothing about what had gone on upstairs when everyone started asking questions. I just sat there listening to them and gasping at the story. I was so thankful they bought it, despite Freddie laughing at me, knowing what really happened.

After all the seeking was completed and people hiding were found, another round was arranged. However, I decided to head home as I didn't want to cause any more damage than I already had!

The first full week of uni passed. I had managed to attend a few lectures and I was slowly getting into a routine – wake up at about 11:00, eat badly cooked food, open a text book and read half a page before deciding I needed to eat again. When it came to cooking I thought I was pretty terrible. Beans and toast was not my limitation but anything further than burnt chicken breast with rice and peas was a push. However, I was in no way as bad as Frank. He would eat the same microwave meals every day, each of them full of fat and doing no good for his body. I was going to ask him why he never cooked when one day I walked in on him in the kitchen with a pan and some ingredients by the hob.

I sat down at the kitchen table with my laptop but I had no intention of logging on, I was simply using it as an excuse to sit there and see what happened. So, like an avid bird watcher finally getting the chance to see the animal he had been searching for his whole life, I sat and stared in silence as Frank tried to muster up some food for himself.

It started off rather well. The hob was turned on and beans were added to the pan. Nothing unusual about that and I started to wonder if I had jumped to the wrong conclusion in thinking Frank couldn't cook.

Unfortunately for Frank, my conclusion was quickly backed up.

Shortly, after adding the beans to the pan, Frank cracked open two eggs and added them to the mixture. I had never seen this technique used before and neither, I think, has anybody else. However, instead of intervening, I continued to observe mesmerised – like a child watching a magic trick for the first time. To my amazement, Frank then picked up two slices of bread, but instead of placing them in the toaster, he placed them on top of the eggs and beans on the pan. It was at this point I had to intervene.

"Erm, Frank, what are you doing, mate?"

"Cooking, what does it look like?"

"It's a funny looking recipe."

"No, it's a simple one."

"Well, I've never seen it before."

"You're telling me you have never had eggs and beans on toast?"

"Not like that, I haven't!"

After about ten minutes of politely explaining the "traditional" way of cooking beans and eggs on toast to Frank, I was told I was wrong and he proceeded to eat the mess that he had already made, at the table next to me.

Having completely finished, he stood up, smiling at me and then proceeded to throw up all over the floor. Amazingly, it looked better once it came back up than it did on his plate.

Chapter 4:

A few more days passed and, despite being able to avoid the "freshers' flu" at the beginning of the year, I woke this particular morning at the usual time, but that day something didn't feel right. I felt ill and when I say ill I mean like *really* ill – I was hardly able to move. Everything ached and my chest felt heavy with whatever infection it was that rested within it.

The funny thing was that, despite my pain and clearly being in need of medical assistance, I couldn't bring myself to ring the doctors. Much like many of you reading this, I am sure that when you fell ill when you were younger, your parents were the ones to phone up and call the doctors for you. Well, I was in that boat, my parents had always sorted my medical appointments so when it came to dealing with it by myself, I had no idea what to do – what bastards my parents were for always helping me!

I lay in bed, staring at the ceiling, my nose was completely blocked and I was having to breathe through my mouth to suck in air.

Layla knocked on my room door and came in. "Christ, you look awful," she said.

"My will is on my desk, you guys can have my overdraft," I joked.

"At least you haven't lost your sense of humour," she laughed. "You do seriously need to get help though."

Layla was right, I did need help. Despite not wanting to organise the appointment myself, I reluctantly looked up the medical centre number on my phone and rang them.

"Hello, University Medical Centre, how can I help?" the woman on the phone asked.

"Hello," I groaned. "I don't want to exaggerate, but I think I might be dying."

I thought she would get the sarcasm, but alarmingly she asked if I was having a heart attack and required an ambulance! After explaining I was only joking and an ambulance would be a considerable waste of time and money, she booked me in for an appointment with the doctor in thirty minutes time.

Knowing it would take me at least twenty minutes from door to door, I heaved myself out of bed and got changed into some comfy tracksuits and jumper. With my legs feeling like jelly, I dragged myself along the corridor and out of the front door and headed for the bus station. To my relief, I arrived just as a bus pulled up and I hopped on to get a lift to the other campus.

I must have looked like death as I had two seats to myself despite it being packed.

I wandered into the medical centre with my nose conveniently starting to run excessively just as I arrived. I fumbled around in my pockets for a tissue but had none on me. I reluctantly had to use my sleeve to clear the residue hanging from my nose, which made me feel even worse. What is it with noses and the way they behave? Mine had gone from being completely blocked to the Niagara Falls in the space of literally thirty seconds.

"Hello, I have an appointment under the name Luke Fagg," I sniffed.

The receptionist stared at me, obviously remembering the awkward phone call earlier on where I joked about dying. She typed away on her keyboard before giving me a nod and telling me to wait in the room at the end of the corridor, gesturing at a bright green door.

I went to say, "Thank you," but before I could, I sneezed.

It came out of nowhere.

Complete normality – then an explosion.

It's common knowledge that you close your eyes when you sneeze and in hindsight, I wish mine had never reopened. As my eyelids rose, I saw the receptionist sat stock still with terror etched all over her face, but it wasn't just terror I was seeing. I hadn't put my hands in the way of my nose as I sneezed and as a consequence snot was now trickling down her left cheek.

"Oh my *God*!" she screamed, fluttering her hands in front of her, unsure what to do.

"I am so, so sorry! I didn't mean to. Please forgive me!" I pleaded.

"You are an idiot, this is so not funny. I can't believe it!"

"You could even say it's *snot* funny," I said.

To this day, I don't know why I made that joke. I mean, number one, it was probably one of the most inappropriate things to say at that point in time and number two, it wasn't even that funny. I can also totally understand the receptionist's reaction as she rose from her chair and bellowed at me to get out of her sight and wait for the doctor until called.

It's fair to say I didn't need telling twice.

I sat there twiddling my thumbs thinking over the terrible event that just unfolded.

"Mr Fagg," the doctor called.

Relieved to be getting seen and closer to getting away from the receptionist, I got up and followed the doctor to his room where he examined me. Turns out I needed antibiotics for a week and I was not able to drink while on them.

Well, that's great, I thought to myself. *I've just snot-rocketed the receptionist and now I can't even drink to forget the awful event.*

I thanked the doctor and, with my prescription in hand, I popped to the pharmacy next door to collect my medication. Given the events that just happened, I joined the queue making sure I had a hand ready to cover my nose in case another sneeze crept up on me. I slowly made my way forward until I was at the front of the queue. Handing over the note, I only had to wait a little time before the pharmacist came back with a small pack of tablets for me. I gratefully paid for the goods and made my way back to the bus stop.

On the way home, I sat down next to a lovely looking red-haired girl. However, before I could introduce myself properly, she immediately got to her feet and sat at the other end of the bus to get as far away from me as possible.

After making no new friends on the bus, I walked back to my flat, took my dose of medicine and went straight to my bed where I instantly fell asleep.

Chapter 5:

I woke the next morning after sleeping sixteen hours straight and feeling a lot better for it. I decided that despite feeling better, I still was not quite well enough to attend my lectures for the day – a decision that obviously took a long time to make. However, it wasn't long before I wished I actually was in a lecture as I quickly became bored lying in my bed.

I texted Anna, asking what she was doing and it wasn't long before there was a knock at the door and she walked in.

"You look better."

"I feel it, I'm just so bored," I replied.

"What about a movie?"

"I think I have watched more movies since I started uni than in the rest of my lifetime."

"Well, what about Tinder? That kills time for me when I'm bored."

"Tinder? What's that?"

"Blimey, you are really behind the times, aren't you? It's a dating app."

Minutes later, I was on Tinder. I had selected what I thought was my best picture and had given a funny and brief description of myself. "Law trainee who enjoys romantic walks to Dominos."

I started swiping left and right through the different girl's profiles with the help of Anna. Like my mother, she sat next to me, quickly pointing out if anything looked wrong with any of the girls we were looking at. Anyone with a spelling mistake in their bio was straight out the door and as for anyone with a name like Crystal, well, you can forget it.

Three hours later – yes, that's right, *three* (I was that desperate) – I still had no match.

Anna offered her motherly support, saying that it wouldn't be long till some nutter matched with me.

The truth was, though, that through the course of the day there was still no luck. To be frank, I was actually both quite pissed off and demoralised.

Luckily, I was presented with the chance to make myself feel better when Freddie came back from his lectures and broke the news that a flat in the halls opposite to us was having a party and we were all invited. I quickly jumped at the opportunity to lift my spirits and made my way down to the student union shop to purchase some alcohol – completely ignoring the doctor's advice about the antibiotics.

Despite feeling awful just the day before, I convinced myself that I felt good enough to attend this party. Deep down, though, I knew it was a terrible idea and it was likely that I would have to leave early as my body wouldn't be able to hack it. Plus, I didn't know how my body would react to the mixture of alcohol and medicine.

Back at the flat and after a quick scrub up, I went to have some beers with the others in the kitchen to kill enough time to be fashionably late to the party. I was keeping tabs on myself and how I was feeling as I took in more drink, but I really didn't feel any different to any other night, which was good news. I was becoming tipsy, but that was it.

At 22:00 we left the flat and made our way over to the gathering. The flat was busy with about thirty people squashed like sardines into the kitchen with lots of drinks in hands. On making my way to the fridge in the corner of the room, I immediately caught sight of a brunette girl. She was very cute. I pointed her out to Freddie and he agreed she was a very attractive girl. Drawing on experiences back in my home town, I knew I wasn't confident with girls and would never have thought I would have a shot with a good-looking girl, but this was uni and I wanted to change that.

Despite this new mind set of wanting to change my approach to girls, I immediately positioned myself as far away from the girl as possible as all the confidence I thought I had never emerged. I ended up chatting to random people who were from the flat next door. But the truth was I wasn't interested in anything they had to say, as my entire focus was working out how I was going to grow a pair of testicles and speak to this brunette girl.

Drink, I thought to myself, *just drink more. Alcohol gives people courage they otherwise wouldn't have and courage was what I need right now*. With that I quickly sloshed down two bottles.

Ten minutes later, I made my move. I was full of confidence. I thought it was the drink doing this, but the medication must have started to kick in, too. Things were becoming more blurry and I was slightly slurring my words, but I was still holding everything together.

We chatted for ages and it wasn't long before I took down her number. Some more chat later and to my surprise, she suggested we go somewhere more private. A sudden realisation came over me that I might have actually pulled! We made our way out of the kitchen to the corridor where we started talking about our shared love of football, of all things. We debated how the season was going to pan out and who the stand out signing had been so far. I disagreed with nearly everything she was saying, but being a man and thinking too much about what could lie ahead, I listened and nodded, backing up whatever comment she came out with. She could have told me Hitler was a great role model and I would have agreed, thinking entirely with my penis.

Time really flew by as we continued to small talk in the corridor – that is until she asked me what my flat was like. I explained it was pretty much the same as the one we were in. She asked if my room was the same too and if she could have a look. Being the naive and stupid idiot I was, I totally missed what she was hinting at and said I would show her despite insisting that it was pretty much the same as hers, bar a few posters, etc.

As we made our way out of the party, she grabbed me by the front door and kissed me. I was shocked at the sudden move she made, but kissed her back. As she pulled away, she grabbed my hand and started walking me towards my flat. It was then the penny finally dropped that this could be *the* night. I thought I might get a kiss after all my grafting, but I never thought it would lead to more ...

As we walked our way over to my flat, I looked back at the party where Freddie gave me a thumbs up from the flat window.

"Go on, my boy!" he shouted after me as I put my arm around my new companion.

With everyone still out, we had the place to ourselves and as soon as the door shut behind us, we kissed one another. We bundled into my room, ripping each other's clothes off.

Soon I was stood there completely naked, as was she.

I felt very nervous, but tried not to let on as I bundled through my drawers to find a condom. I was all about losing my virginity but in no mood to become a dad at the same time.

She lay herself on my bed and urged me to join her. I positioned myself on top of her and we started kissing again.

I quickly glanced at the clock – 23:24.

Freddie had always said, "It's not about the size of the wave but the motion of the ocean and how long those waves ride for."

Don't rush, I thought to myself, *for God's sake don't rush and be a disappointment*.

It was at that moment that it all began and it felt as good as I had imagined.

After what felt like the time of my life and feeling very satisfied with myself, I looked back over at the clock – 23:24.

What the *fuck*? *It must be broken*, I thought to myself. Click. 23:25. Oh, come on! Not even one minute, that's shocking!

"Are you done?" said a voice underneath me.

"Errrmmm," I stumbled.

She laughed. "Don't worry, it happens to everyone."

Thankfully, despite experiencing possibly one of the worst sexual performances (who am I kidding – it was *the* worst) she had ever come across, she had a sense of humour and she didn't bolt out of the room, laughing her way back home. Instead, she sat up and we began to chat again. It was surprisingly easy for us to get on and with no awkward silences, we both found ourselves laughing and enjoying each other's company very much. However, after an hour and it getting late, she understandably said it was probably best she made a move.

She unwrapped the duvet from around her and popped on her clothes as I wrestled a pair of boxers on under the covers, embarrassed that she might see me naked again. As she got up to make her way out, I stopped her.

Thinking about how well we got on, I decided to make another move.

"Listen, I'm sorry about my performance, but I was wondering, would you want to meet up again for a drink or something?" I asked timidly.

"Yeah, sure," she smiled.

"Great!" I said in a much higher pitch than I intended. "Well, can I grab your number, then?" I asked.

"You already have it," she laughed. "Look it up."

It was then that an awful feeling passed over my body.

Not only had I just forgotten this girl had given me her number, I had now realised I couldn't look it up as I had forgotten her name. I thought quickly about what to do next. She didn't know I had forgotten her name, just that I had forgotten I had taken down her number. So, I just had to play it off and I would be okay.

Well, I tried and she saw straight through me.

"If you remember taking it down, look it up," she demanded.

I froze.

With a glare on her face, she stomped past me, picked up my phone from my desk and handed it to me. I hesitated before tapping in my password. I purposely went into my Facebook app and then my Instagram as a ploy to waste time before looking up my contacts list. I delayed as much as possible before it became obvious I was stalling and did not have a clue what her name really was.

"Listen, I'm sorry," I pleaded, knowing my fate.

"I knew it!" she shouted.

She began screaming at me and telling me I was just like any other guy and only had one thing on my mind.

That one thing certainly isn't your name, I thought to myself.

I was about to tell her to leave out of embarrassment, when I suddenly remembered the old saying – "The best form of defence is attack."

"Hang on ... What's my name, then?" I asked, almost pleased with myself.

"Luke," she snapped.

"Fuck. That backfired," I muttered. Now I really was in a bad situation. Clutching at straws, I asked her what letter her name began with, desperate to try to salvage the sorry state of affairs.

"Why would I give you that?" she barked at me.

"I promise I will remember if you tell me the first letter!"

After what felt like an eternity, she kindly gave in and told me this was my last chance.

"It begins with the letter Y," she said.

Of all the bloody letters in the alphabet but a Y. What bloody girl's name begins with a Y? Was she foreign? Was it Russian or something? No, she was from Southampton, I remembered that. Okay, so she was from Southampton and it began with a Y. I racked my brain, but nothing was coming to mind. I tried to think of famous actors or public figures to spark something.

She folded her arms and I knew I was about to run out of time.

"Errmmm, Yolanda?" I asked. Yolanda? Yo-*fucking*-Landa. Of all the names I could have guessed? I went for that! Is it even a name?

She didn't have to shout to show how angry she was, she just looked deep into my eyes, rage spreading across her face. She reached out and slapped me hard across my right cheek. It was so painful it gave Andy's hit, earlier in the year, a run for its money. She then stormed out of my room before slamming the door in my face.

I opened the door to chase after her into the corridor, feeling unbelievably guilty and ashamed with myself. Outside my room, I was greeted by the rest of my flat all stood in the corridor with faces of horror. The front door slammed and I let out a sigh of despair as I heard her tear off down the stairs and out of sight, shouting to herself and cursing me.

"Things didn't go well with Yasmin, then?" Freddie asked.

Yasmin– that was it.

The name that will forever haunt me. I slumped to the floor and held my head in my hands. How had that all gone so wrong so quickly?

"I lasted less than a minute in bed and then forgot her name," I confessed to the others as I rested the back of my head up against the wall.

Silence filled the corridor until a snigger came from Layla. This triggered a chain reaction and it wasn't long before they were all rolling around on the floor laughing at what had just happened. I started laughing, too – as bad as it had been, I could see the funny side too.

A little later I looked in my contacts of my phone and there it was – Yasmin. I thought about dropping her a text to apologise, but thought better of it. Probably best to let things die down a bit and then I could drop her a message next year or something …

Chapter 6:

During the first couple of weeks at university, you sort of forget all the little homely things you take for granted. You are too busy settling into your new life. But as you begin to become more accustomed to the daily routine of university, you start to miss things like a roast on a Sunday or just a chat with your mum and dad. The truth is, you can become a little bit homesick and this is exactly what happened to Layla and Anna in my flat. They just wanted to see their parents and siblings and so made a journey back home for a weekend. This left just Freddie, Frank and I in the flat and so we needed to come up with an idea to keep ourselves entertained. And so, we got together for a group meeting and started brainstorming ideas in the kitchen.

At first we sat in silence, all three of us swinging on the back legs of our chairs, thinking about what we could do with the two free days.

"The pub is always an option to watch the football?" Freddie suggested.

"Yeah, but that's not really an evening thing," I replied.

Silence fell between us again before Freddie's phone pinged. He picked it up and a smile spread across his face.

"Lads, we've just been handed the solution to our problems!" He grinned.

"You just got a discount code for Dominos?" Frank said, leaning forward.

"What? No." Freddie laughed.

He explained to us that a long term friend of his had just invited him to her birthday party in London and plus ones (or twos, in our case) were welcome. He quickly fired a text back to her and confirmed we would all be attending!

With the plan for the night coming together, we popped off to our rooms to pack an overnight bag and then hopped down the road to pick up some drinks. Alongside my usual alcohol purchase, I also bought a bottle of wine for the hosts. I was always told by my parents that when being a guest, you should bring something for the hosts as, after all, they are the ones inviting you into their house and the ones who are going to have to clean whatever mess may be left in the morning. A bottle of wine, although only small, can make the tidy up feel just that little bit better.

A short tube and taxi ride later, the three of us rocked up to the house at about 21:00. As we stood outside, we were greeted by a tall, white building with giant concrete pillars stood either side of a huge black door. Every house on the street had the same front and each had a different type of expensive car parked outside it. Ferraris, Maseratis and Porches all lined the pavement, each painted a more extravagant colour than the next.

We walked up the five concrete steps to the front door and could hear noise coming from inside.

"This is easily the biggest house I have ever seen," gasped Frank, staring up to the four stories above us.

"I told you she was minted!" laughed Freddie.

He grabbed the round, silver door knocker and hit it against the door three times.

A couple of seconds later, the door swung round to reveal a beautiful, petite woman stood in front of us.

"Freddie!" she shouted, holding out her arms and then embracing him in a big hug.

"It's so good to see you, Emily," he said, putting his arms round her.

As she rested her chin on his shoulder, I could see just how beautiful she was. A cute, round face with little dimples as she smiled. Her long, curly red hair was down and complimented the explosion of blue that lit up her dazzling eyes. She looked over Freddie's shoulder and made eye contact with me.

I instantly smiled.

"You must be Luke or Frank?" she asked.

"Luke," I quickly replied with a smile across my face.

She leant forward and gave Frank and I a quick hug each before inviting us in.

The hallway was grand and immaculately clean. The white décor contrasted the beautiful black, figure hugging dress Emily wore. People were stood against each of the walls drinking and gave us three newcomers a nod as we made our way towards the back of the house where the kitchen was.

"Welcome to the party, guys," said Emily, presenting a huge array of alcohol on the kitchen worktop. "Feel free to put your stuff in the guest room on the third floor – it's the one on the left – and other than that feel free to help yourselves to the BBQ and make yourselves at home!"

"Thank you," we all replied at the same time.

And with that, Emily turned and made her way outside where we could see about fifty people all gathered around chatting with a DJ spinning away in the background.

Freddie, knowing the house best out of all of us, led the way upstairs to our room.

We made our way back down the hallway and took the stairs up to the floors above. The soft white carpet cushioned each one of my steps and I couldn't help but feel guilty I might be getting them dirty with my shoes still on. Three flights of stairs later and we arrived at our floor.

Freddie held out a finger and pointed at the door on the left-hand side of the corridor. "Our bedroom." He then gestured to the one furthest down the corridor. "Bathroom." Before pointing at the door closest to us. "Her grandmother's room."

"Perfect," I said, repeating what he had told us in my head.

We made our way into our room. It was enormous. On the far wall was a king sized bed covered with cushions and a red blanket laid across the foot of it. Behind it, the wall was covered with a gold patterned wallpaper. On the right-hand side lay a sofa, which Freddie explained turned into another double bed. We all looked at each other before sprinting towards the king sized bed.

I was first to arrive.

Shouting shotgun, I threw myself in amongst the pillows.

Freddie cursed at his slow reactions and the fact he had missed out.

At the same time, Frank had made his way over to the sofa bed, which left Freddie stranded. Knowing how unfair it would be to let him sleep on the floor, I offered for us to top and tail. Freddie laughed and took up my offer, whilst at the same time pointing out that we would not even have anything to do if it wasn't for him – which was very true!

With sleeping arrangements made, I popped my bag on the bed and unzipped it. Inside, I had a bottle of vodka and two bottles of lemonade along with the wine as well as a change of clothes and some Paul Smith aftershave – which in my opinion is one of the best smelling out there. I took off my t-shirt, folded it on the bed and took my very best blue shirt out of my bag. I buttoned it up and looked around me to see the other guys doing exactly the same. A quick splash of the aftershave and I was ready.

"Let's do this!" I said, clapping my hands together, eager to get involved with the party.

The others joined me at the door and we made our way down the corridor looking like we were about to take to the stage as the world's worst boyband.

We arrived back at the kitchen. The music was louder than before and the atmosphere was building, but I had only one thing in my head – I wanted to get to know Emily and try my best to get her number. I may not get the chance to meet her again and so I needed to take my opportunity to speak to her and get to know her as best I could while making a good impression. I knew that to do that I had to ensure I did not forget her name.

However, in order to get talking to her, I needed to pluck up some courage. Solution? Liquid courage of course.

I got together three red cups and poured out three vodka lemonades. I handed one each to Freddie and Frank and we touched cups.

"Here's to a good night!" Freddie smirked.

We took a sip before all pulling the same screwed up face as we realised how strong I had made them.

Looking around to see who to mingle with, we heard a huge cheer from behind us. A game of beer pong was going on and by the look of it, somebody must have just sunk a shot. I looked across at Freddie and Frank. They could tell from the look in my eye what I wanted. I made my way out of the patio doors and towards the iconic drinking game with my two mates following behind. I knew I was good at beer pong – in fact, in all the times I had played it, I had never lost. A genuine fact.

Our arrival at the table was good timing, the cheer had been for the winning shot and the successful team were looking for new opponents.

"We'll take you on," I said, stepping out at the end of the table with Freddie and Frank stood either side of me.

"You're on!" a guy in a black t-shirt shouted back to me.

Each team filled their cups with different alcohol and a small crowd gathered around us.

"They haven't lost in four games," said a gentle voice behind me.

I turned to see Emily and I couldn't help but smile at seeing her again.

"Well, best we end that winning run then!" I winked in a terribly cringey fashion.

The opposition went first and sunk with their first shot.

"Boom!" was the cry and there were high fives all round.

I stepped forward and picked the ball out of the liquid before downing the drink.

I looked up and positioned myself before firing the ball back at the opposition's cups. Plop. I high fived my team and was taken aback when Emily gave me a hug.

The next two shots from the opposition both missed. Freddie missed his, too, but Frank didn't.

We were winning.

With that, the guy in black stepped forward and sank his shot again.

Praise of, "Nice one, Gary!" was shouted out behind him. With that shot from Gary, we were tied at four all.

I threw back. Plop. Make that three cups left for us to get.

The crowd continued to gather around us, sensing there could be an upset on the cards. The frustration was spreading in the opposition team and with more misses from them and another two successful throws from us, we were left with one cup and they were still left with four. You could sense desperation in the opposition as they started to try and put me off before I had even been handed the ball.

"You've just been lucky!" shouted Gary above the noise of everyone else.

I looked over my shoulder as I picked up the ball from the table. Emily was still looking and I took that as my moment to stand out.

I turned and looked Gary directly in the eye. Without breaking eye contact, I threw the ball.

It cut its way through the air.

I didn't even see it land in the cup as I still stared it out with Gary, but the roar of the crowd let me know we had won.

I held my arms out as wide as I could as people swarmed around me, jumping up and down in celebration, like we had just brought the World Cup home.

Across the table, I could see the disappointment on Gary and his teammates' faces, but it was only a bit of fun at the end of the day and they were quick to give our team a thumbs up.

The hype of the moment quickly died down, but I still felt great about what had just happened.

Emily was stood next to me and I took the moment to ask, "Drink to celebrate that victory?"

"Yeah, sure!" she replied. "Let me just get Gary."

Why would she want Gary to come? I thought to myself when the penny suddenly dropped.

She wandered back a few seconds later clutching Gary by his arm.

"Fair play, mate, you took my beer pong crown and for a second thought you were gonna take my girl," he laughed.

I shook his hand and smiled. "Thanks, mate! Don't worry, she's all yours!" I laughed, looking over at Emily.

The truth was, I was gutted.

I had got myself so worked up into some sort of Hollywood fantasy, I genuinely thought I had a chance with Emily, and although Gary had done nothing wrong and seemed like a top bloke, it didn't stop me from wanting to take my vodka bottle and shove it where the sun don't shine.

Before I could get into any deep conversation with the happy couple, I got a tap on the shoulder. Freddie was stood behind me and invited me inside. Without hesitation, I accepted, happy to escape my role as a third wheel. Inside, he apologised for not telling me Emily had a boyfriend and letting me waste my time.

I laughed at how apologetic he was – it wasn't as if I had spent hours chasing after her, it had been all of an hour! I still appreciated his explanation, though, I was just a little disappointed, that's all. Despite explaining this all to Freddie, he was still apologetic and explained he had an idea to cheer me up. After a quick trip upstairs, he came back holding a bottle of tequila.

As with every party you go to, a full bottle of alcohol quickly attracted other people and it wasn't long before we were doing shots with about ten other people. I tried to take it slow, knowing that tequila usually didn't agree with me, but you know how it is and I was quickly peer pressured into having shot after shot.

Before long, we had nearly finished the bottle.

A huge sense of relief spread across my body as the bottle ran out just as they were coming around to pour my final shot and, despite the others' insistence, I managed to wriggle out of doing another.

Feeling a little fragile, I decided to make myself a vodka lemonade to get the tequila taste out of my mouth. I made it as weak as possible in the hope of avoiding getting a spinning head as the night went on.

A couple of hours later, my plan had not worked. My head was all over the place as I joined everyone out in the garden to dance away to the DJ's tracks. It was a beautiful night, just the right temperature to be outside and with the BBQ in the corner, if you did end up feeling a little cold you could pop over and warm yourself up while munching on a burger.

It seemed that, despite my earlier efforts of making my vodka lemonade as weak as possible and trying to line my stomach with food, I still found my head spinning every time I closed my eyes and I couldn't work out why.

I found Freddie to tell him and to my surprise he told me he was actually pouring vodka into my drink when I wasn't looking as he knew I was avoiding making them too strong.

I don't know how he had managed to do it so sneakily, but it had certainly worked and I was very unsteady on my feet. Seeing that he had perhaps gone too far with his joke, Freddie suggested I went to the sitting room and had a sit down before I headed up to bed.

Taking his advice on board, I poured myself a glass of water and took a seat on one of the comfy leather sofas in the lounge. There was nobody else in the room, so I sat there quietly, trying to take back control of my intoxicated body while sipping at my cup of water. I gently slapped my cheek to try to spring some life into me, but it only had a short term affect and before long a combination of alcohol and tiredness got the better of me.

A while later, I woke up in a complete daze.

I glanced around, trying to take in my surroundings. I was still alone in the room which I then realised was covered in empty bottles and cups, including the bottle of tequila Freddie had brought out earlier in the evening. I rummaged around for my phone in my pocket and clicked the home button.

My eyes had to adjust themselves to the bright screen before I could read the time.

04:17.

"Bloody *hell*," I muttered to myself, how long had I been out for?

I sat up and cupped my head in my hands and closed my eyes. It was then that the realisation of just how drunk I was set in.

The room span and I had to quickly open my eyes before the feeling of sickness came over me too strongly. I took a moment to take some short, deep breaths, but the feeling of sickness was beginning to take a hold. I needed to lie down and so I rolled over on my side. My shirt instantly absorbed whatever liquid it was that had soaked into the cushions I was lying on and the smell of alcohol filled my nostrils. The pungent odour was too much for my senses to bear.

I was going to be sick.

As quick as I could, I got to my feet. I had one thing on my mind – get to the toilet. Still hazy, I stumbled along the hallway and made my way to the bottom of the stairs. I lifted my foot to begin the ascent, but caught the top of the first step. Alcohol had slowed down my body considerably and as a result my arms offered no help in breaking my fall. Instead, my forehead took the full whack of the steps.

Bang.

"Fuck it!" I cursed.

With the accumulation of my stomach and now my sore head, I really felt unwell and I could feel whatever it was inside me making its way up my body. I heaved myself to my feet using the banister beside me and restarted my climb.

Clinging to the handrail with every step, I eventually made it to the third floor and spotted the bathroom at the far end. Relief set in as I realised how close I was. I sprinted towards it and went to turn the handle. It wouldn't budge. I tried again, this time harder, but still no movement.

"Oh, come *on*," I grunted, throwing my head back in frustration.

I looked back down the corridor in desperation and suddenly had a brain wave. Our room didn't have a toilet, but did the grandmother's room Freddie had pointed out earlier have one? I took a few quick steps with my stomach rumbles getting ever louder.

As I got to the door, it all became too much and suddenly I felt liquid surge up my throat. I covered my mouth with my hand and without hesitation burst into the grandmother's room. Thankfully, there was nobody in the room, but unfortunately there was no toilet either!

I looked around for anything I could use as liquid began to seep between my fingers. I span around frantically before spotting a vase on the mantelpiece above the fireplace.

I ran over, took off the lid and threw up inside. I breathed short and shallow breaths while placing an arm against the mantelpiece to steady myself. I felt a lot better and, knowing I wasn't going to be sick again, I put the lid back on the vase.

The vase itself was large and had a beautiful blue pattern across it. I felt terribly guilty looking at it, knowing what I had just done, but in truth was more thankful I had been sick in it rather than on the bed or carpet. I placed it gently back to its original positon, but knew I couldn't leave it the way it was and would have to wash it out. Plus, I would have to get it cleaned before anyone else woke up and caught me in the act.

All of sudden, I heard movement in the corridor. It was coming from up towards the toilet.

I crept slowly over to the bedroom door and pulled it tenderly ajar before peeking through the gap. There, I saw Freddie staggering his way back to the bedroom.

"Hey," I whispered.

Freddie looked around him, bemused as to where the noise had come from.

"Over here," I whispered again.

He saw my face in the little gap of the door and made his way over to me as I ushered him inside.

"This is her grandmother's room, what are you doing in here?" he asked, shutting the door behind him.

I explained to him that I had felt sick and because he was using the toilet, I had been sick in this room instead as I had no time to find somewhere else.

He looked around the room, baffled by the fact there was no toilet and yet I had made no mess either. "You must have cleaned it up pretty well!" Freddie laughed. "Do you carry Vanish around with you everywhere you go?"

I laughed and explained to him that I hadn't actually cleaned it up yet and that was my next job, gesturing at vase above the fireplace.

Freddie's faced dropped.

"What?" I asked anxiously.

Freddie stared at me, then at the vase, then back at me.

"*What*?" I asked more loudly as my anxiousness grew.

"Luke, although this is Emily's grandmother's room, she doesn't actually live here."

"Okay, great, so I have time to sort out cleaning it all then, before she gets back."

"No, Luke. The grandmother isn't alive anymore. She's actually *in* that vase."

My heart skipped a beat as I twigged what he meant. "You're fucking kidding me. You mean to say that in that vase is her grandmother's ashes and I have just been sick all over them?"

Freddie nodded.

"Jesus Christ!" I shouted.

"Keep your voice down!" Freddie snapped.

"Oh, I'm sorry, I'll just try and remain calm after finding out I've just vomited tequila over a dead woman's ashes who is the grandmother of a girl I only met tonight! I tell you what, why don't I calmly go and find the grandfather's urn while I'm at it and have a shit in that to complete the package?" I snapped back.

"Her grandfather's actually still alive, so that's not possible."

"Argh!" I grunted angrily.

"Luke, Luke. Okay. I know this is bad, but we need to come up with a plan!"

Chapter 7:

I paced back and forth in the room, trying to get my alcohol-fuddled brain to kick into gear. The time was now 05:00 and we were fast approaching when people would be waking up. As if the throwing up wasn't bad enough, Freddie had now explained to me that Emily's mother had found the whole death of her mother very traumatic. It turns out she used to visit her mother, Gladice, every day but the one day she didn't, Gladice had taken a tumble and was left unconscious at the bottom of the stairs. Emily's mum had blamed herself for her death and thought if she had been there she could have been saved.

Tragically, it filled Emily's mum with terrible guilt and as a result, she would often come into the room and talk to her mum's ashes, asking for forgiveness. This meant that it wouldn't be long before she picked up on the smell of sick coming from the vase.

I threw my arms up in the air. "This is hopeless. I might as well kill myself, you cremate me and then replace my ashes with hers. Then the mum doesn't suspect a thing and I get to escape this whole ordeal!" I moaned.

Freddie held up a hand to stop me talking. "I have an idea," he said, looking up from the bed he was sat on.

"Enlighten me," I replied desperately.

A few seconds later, Freddie creaked open the door.

We had, at most, an hour to sort this godforsaken mess out.

He leant his head out of the room and checked if the corridor was clear. "Okay, we're good," he whispered, waving his hand behind him for me to follow.

I crept after him with the giant blue vase cradled in my arms. We had both taken off our shoes so as to avoid making any more noise than necessary and we also made sure that we put both pairs of our shoes back into our room to avoid leaving any trace of us being in the grandmother's room.

Freddie then led the way as we tip toed to the bathroom. We kept checking over our shoulders as we went, but thankfully there was no sign of anybody else being up.

The sound as we opened the bathroom door seemed impossibly loud, but we made it inside undetected, despite the best efforts of the squeaky hinges to give us away.

"Right, this is the bad part," Freddie confessed.

"What do we need to do?" I quizzed.

"We need to flush all of those contents down the toilet."

"Are you *actually* mental?"

"Luke! We either flush away this dead lady or you leave her mixed in with your vomit like some kind of dead Granny Gladice cocktail for the mum or anyone else to find."

As much as it pained me to admit it, he was right. I would never live it down if anyone found out. In fact, I probably wouldn't live at all because Emily or her mum would probably kill me and then I would end up in a vase of my own propped up somewhere.

I looked down at the vase and hooked my fingers through the handle of the ceramic lid. I couldn't believe what I was doing, but there just didn't seem to be any other option. I pulled on the lid and the most horrendous smell filled the room. Freddie covered his nose and mouth as did I in an attempt to block out the fumes.

I shot Freddie one last look to make sure he knew we were now in this together. He nodded and I tipped the vase forward over the white ceramic toilet bowl.

Out came what can only be described as the worst sight I have ever seen.

A mixture of grey and yellow that had the consistency of cement oozed its way out of the vase. The water in the toilet soon turned a light grey colour, with small bits of sweetcorn floating around that must have come from a meal I ate not long back. It was really grim and the worst part was the amount left stuck to the inside of the vase. With nothing to scrape it off with, I had to use my hand to get most of the remaining mixture out.

Freddie could tell I was struggling and took the vase from my hands. He walked past me to the sink as I sat slumped on the edge of the toilet and began to fill the urn with water. Neither of us said a word as the water rose to halfway. He then sloshed it around like you do with a saucepan, before pouring it down the toilet. He gestured towards the toilet handle, which I gently pushed down on. We watched as the mixture disappeared and was replaced by crystal clear water.

"Right, now we need to fill it with the replacement," whispered Freddie.

"Yeah, you didn't actually say what that was?"

"The ashes from the BBQ."

"*Jesus*," I said, burying my head in my hands.

"It's the only thing I could think of."

"I know, I know, I'm not having a go, I just never thought in a million years I would be replacing a dead woman's ashes with the remains of last night's BBQ," I sighed.

With the next phase of the plan ready, we made some last minute checks in the bathroom to make sure that everything was clean. We even went to the extent of taking a few wet wipes from the cupboard and cleaning some of the surfaces so there was no evidence of us being there, or trace of what we had done.

Freddie leant out of the bathroom door and we started the same process again of checking everything was clear before making our move. We inched our way along the corridor, still constantly listening out for anyone who might be up.

I was holding the vase – we hadn't even had to discuss who should carry it as we both knew had it not been for me, neither of us would be in this mess. The only issue I had was the vase was so big that if we were to bump into anyone, I would have no way of hiding it. We would be caught red handed.

The one bit of luck he did have on our side was the lovely, cushioned carpet, which meant we didn't make a sound all the way down to the hallway.

Freddie had me hold back as he made his way to the sitting room and kitchen to check everything was clear. A thumbs up signalled for me to get moving.

I was quick but careful making my way to the glass patio door where Freddie was stood. He flicked the lock up and began to slide the door across. It was excruciatingly loud as it squealed against the metal frame. With the noise too much to bear, we opened it just enough to squeeze our bodies through.

Freddie went first, breathing in and shuffling sideways like a space invader through the tiny gap.

Then it was my turn.

I carefully passed Freddie the vase and copied his technique. Just as I stuck my front leg forward, I felt a rip on my trousers. I looked down, expecting to see them caught on a nail of some kind, but instead saw a cat clawing away at my leg. I had accidently wedged it between my foot and the door frame while trying to push myself through.

I immediately retracted my leg as the cat hissed at me, still grappling with my trousers. Despite now being back inside, the cat still didn't let go and continued to tear at my leg. I felt a sharp pain as one of its claws ripped into my skin. I bit my lip, knowing I couldn't let out any noise. I shook my leg around like some kind of fast-forwarded version of the okie-cokie as the cat continued to grapple with me.

Freddie whispered at me, angrily telling me to get it off before it caused too much commotion. In a panic, I kicked out my leg as hard as I could. The ginger cat flew through the air and smashed into the glass door, letting out a yelp.

I winced at the noise and felt guilty, but was relieved to see it land on its feet.

With a chance to escape, I quickly raced outside and closed the door behind me. I breathed heavily, standing outside as my body recovered from the rush of what had just happened. Looking back through the glass door, I saw the feline walking up and down by the window, staring both of us out as it did so.

"Stupid ginger prick," I grunted angrily. I never had liked cats and this further reinforced my opinion of them.

Before I had the chance to throw any more insults at the animal, Freddie grabbed my arm and pulled me along the garden to the BBQ.

Without hesitation, we removed the grill and began shovelling ash into the vase as quickly as we could, taking big cupped handfuls at a time. It wasn't long before it reached the same level as its previous contents. We quickly put the grill back the way it was and headed back to the patio doors. Thankfully, the cat had now disappeared from view and we quickly opened the door and made our way inside.

I let out a small sigh of relief, knowing that we were nearly there and had pulled off an almost impossible cover up. We started making our way along the hall and up the stairs when a door suddenly opened on the first floor.

Freddie and I froze and looked at each other.

Realising we might not have much time, we raced back down towards the kitchen as quickly and quietly as we could. Whoever it was upstairs was heading our way and we had very little time for a plan.

In a panic, we opened up the kitchen cupboards to try to find anywhere to put the vase. We literally opened every cupboard available but they were all rammed full of pans, cups and plates.

Suddenly, the footsteps were at the entrance of the kitchen. In a last ditch attempt to hide it, I put the vase on the counter behind me and stood in front of it, angling my body so as to obscure it from the view of whoever it was about to enter.

"Oh, hi, boys," said Emily's mum, walking into the kitchen.

"Hi!" we both replied in unusually high pitched voices.

Standing up against the counter, I made myself as wide as possible, using every inch of my body to try to block the view of the vase.

"Would you like a coffee?" she asked us.

"No thanks, Julie," said Freddie for us both, knowing we needed to get out of there as soon as possible.

Julie then started walking around the kitchen island towards me, looking to grab something out of a cupboard in the corner to my left. Freddie and I looked at each other, our eyes wide with fear, as she brushed past me.

I shuffled my body around with hers as she walked past, changing the positioning of my body to try to cover the new angle she had now created from her movement. However, as you can imagine, this was not a natural look with me stood arching my back over the counter with my arms tight against my sides – it almost looked as if I was posing for some sort of saucy calendar shoot.

Still fearing we may be found out, we made polite small talk as Julie fumbled around in the cupboards to find whatever ingredients she needed to make her cup of coffee and thankfully it wasn't long until she switched the kettle on. Ideas ran through my head, but I had nothing that stood out as a means of escaping. I continued to lean awkwardly against the counter when I saw Freddie slowly make his way to the kitchen entrance. For a second, I feared he may be doing a runner, but thankfully he stopped by the door and mouthed something at me.

At first, I thought I must have read his lips wrong, but as he began to impersonate the throwing of the vase, out of the sight of Julie, I realised he was telling me to chuck it to him so he could hide it further from Emily's mum.

Taking a deep breath, I prepared myself and thought about how I needed to react quickly and also quietly when I had my chance.

Just as I planned my movements, Julie turned to the kettle as it was just about to reach the boil.

I took my chance.

With her back turned, I span around and grabbed the vase in both hands. I then continued to spin and threw it all in one motion to Freddie. To my horror, I realised that I had not put enough force into my throw and could see the vase was going to drop short.

Freddie took a big step forward as I covered my mouth in fear.

To my sheer relief, Freddie caught the vase a couple of centimetres above the floor.

The lid made a rattle as Freddie held tight.

Julie heard the noise and turned to see what was going on, but thankfully Freddie had already pushed the vase around the corner and then covered himself by explaining he was kneeling down to get a stone out of his sock.

She was completely oblivious to what had happened.

Knowing we now had everything in place for our escape back upstairs, we both quickly thanked Julie for the offer of the coffee and then made our excuses to scuttle off upstairs.

We wasted no time in getting back to the grandmother's room and as quick as you like, the urn was back on the mantelpiece above the fireplace, safe and in its original position.

Agreeing to never speak again about what we had just done, we scampered back to our bedroom.

Frank awoke as we entered the room. He looked bemused and asked what we were doing up so early and walking around together.

"Oh, we just gave a hand cleaning up. Felt bad about the mess," I said.

With Frank buying the lie, Freddie and I looked at each other and breathed a subtle sigh of relief.

I felt like the worst person in the world, but only Freddie and I knew how bad the last few hours had been.

I had what can only be described as the quickest shower of my life about five minutes later. I wanted to sort of cleanse myself of the sin I had just committed but also wanted to get out of the house as quickly as possible. We were so desperate to get out of there we even agreed to skip breakfast.

Frank was a little annoyed at first, but thankfully agreed when Freddie and I suggested a greasy fry up on the way home instead. I didn't want to be there any longer than necessary and I could tell from Freddie's face that he didn't either.

We headed downstairs where we found that Emily was also now awake and stood with her mum in the kitchen. After a short chat and reminiscing on the night before and what a great evening it had been, we thanked them both for their hospitality and kindness before making our way to the front door.

The sense of respite as the door shut behind us and we made our way down along the street was one I don't think I have ever experienced before and hope I don't have to experience again. It was almost like overcoming a sickness – it meant that much to be away and out of sight from the tragic events we had just partaken in.

It was a night I will never forget, but wish I could.

Chapter 8:

Now you are probably thinking, "In amongst all these events of losing his virginity and washing away dead people, is he actually getting any work done?" Well, the truth is, yes!

But, that did not necessarily make it *good* work as I found out getting marks back for three pieces of coursework I had done. Results of forty-two, forty-five and forty-six were nothing to be proud of. Although a pass, that's all they were and I felt I was doing myself no favours paying all this money and not actually bothering to get a decent grade.

I was about three months into uni and on receiving these marks; I decided it was time to really put a bit more effort in. So from that day, instead of just lazing about when I got home from lectures, I decided to actually write up the notes I had taken onto revision cards, which I could look back on from time to time. The great thing was that, after doing this for a while, I realised it did not eat into any time that was important to me, just time that I would have spent lying on my bed literally doing nothing.

I was slowly becoming more interactive during lectures and, dare I say it, feeling more intelligent. But that newfound intelligence didn't stop me from enjoying the less intellectual, but nevertheless important, life lesson conversations.

I had come back to the flat on this particular day to find Freddie and Frank in the kitchen deep in conversation.

"But a girl likes it if it's not messy down there," pressed Freddie.

"Yeah, I know, I just mean that you don't have to be clean shaven," retorted Frank.

Naturally, I asked what they were on about. Simple, really, does a girl prefer hair in the downstairs areas of a man, or do they prefer him clean shaven? It was a hotly debated topic and one I was instantly drawn into.

We bickered about the pros and cons. I mean, it can be great having less hair down there but it makes you look like a teen who hasn't hit puberty yet and it can be precarious at times to manage.

The debate raged on before Frank and Freddie were quick to point out that I had no facial hair whatsoever. This was true. Despite being nineteen I did not have a single hair on my face. They both had thick stubble and could, if they wanted, grow a full beard. They quizzed me as to whether I had hair anywhere else on my body considering how bare my face was.

I joked that my bottom probably had the most, to which they both laughed.

They then asked if I had ever thought about doing anything about it.

I was quite shocked by the question. I had never considered it a real area of importance – I mean, after all, it's hardly like it's visible. Even if I were naked I would like to think I would be facing someone and talking to them rather than having my back to them bent over. To my amazement, though, both Frank and Freddie explained that they waxed theirs to keep them all tidy.

Freddie recommended I sorted it early with Frank nodding in agreement. Apparently, the earlier you get a hold over it the better?

Well, after having a very in depth discussion, I found myself five minutes later knocking on Anna's door. We had heard the girl's talking about waxing their legs before so we were sure she would have some waxing strips – which Anna did. However, we obviously did not want to let on what we were going to use the waxing strips for and so agreed amongst ourselves that we were going to say I had lost a dare and had to wax my legs as a punishment. A good cover story and one that Anna did not question.

Frank and Freddie told me to go back to my room, read through the instructions very carefully and then come back to the kitchen when the deed was done, which in hindsight was a bit weird. Most mates might ask you to tell them about your first try at a cigarette once you've had it – I was going to tell them about my first "manscaping" exhibition.

I locked my door and stood in my room and read the instructions twice just to make sure I had got them right.

Simple, really.

Expose the area of concern. Warm the strip up by placing on a radiator and then place it on that area. Leave it about ten to fifteen minutes for the wax to set and finally rip off in a quick, firm motion.

The first problem I had was exposing the area. I stripped off from the waist down and tried lying on my back first. Definite no, I couldn't get comfortable and knew a slip up could leave me in all sorts of problems. Then I tried resting a leg on the edge of my desk like some kind of ballet dancer warm up. At first it seemed a good idea, but then I realised my standing leg would quickly tire and I would have to readjust my position. I eventually decided on squatting. Although it could be a struggle holding a squat for ten minutes, it was the only real way I could find that worked and it shared the workload between my legs. I debated sitting down, but the problem was any excess wax that leaked could mean I became stuck to the chair.

With the plan set, I spread my legs and adopted a sumo sort of stance. I then took the strip and placed it along the crevice of my bottom. The second the gel touched my behind I could feel it grip my hairs. It was strong and I instantly could tell it was going to take some force to rip it off a little later on.

Then the waiting began.

The ten minutes felt like an eternity, but eventually the timer I had set on my phone went off. On previous experiences of pulling off plasters, I knew that it was imperative that when I pulled on this strip I did so with as much force and speed as possible in order for it all to be over in a flash. I couldn't afford to give it a gentle tug, doing that would drag out the whole painful process.

I reached between my legs and grabbed the strip at the rear of my bum.

"Okay," I said to myself. "You can do this. Three ... two ... one and a half ... one ... and ..." I was just about to pull when the fire alarm suddenly went off. It gave me such a fright that I immediately leapt to my feet.

This was the worst possible thing to do.

While squatting, my buttocks had been somewhat separated from one another, however, in standing up, they were now in contact and, although, the pack said the gel took ten to fifteen minutes to set, it was still sticky and this had essentially resulted in my arse being welded shut.

In desperation, I lifted my right leg outwards to try to peel my right cheek from my left cheek, but the grip on the skin was so strong it just caused an unbelievable amount of pain.

I heard Anna shout from the corridor that we all had to evacuate as quickly as possible.

"Fuck, fuck, fuck!" I grunted, angrily scurrying around trying to think what to do.

I grabbed the handle of my door in a panic to get a move on and then remembered I was half naked. I hopped with my two feet together to my tracksuit bottoms on the end of my bed and wriggled around, trying to get my feet in the correct trouser legs. It was a nightmare but, after doing my best impression of a worm, I squeezed them over my knees and yanked them up to my waist. Fully dressed, I snatched open the door and hopped my way down the corridor, unable to walk properly due to my bottom's new accessory.

I looked out the window by the front door and could see that everyone else was already out of the flat and outside the main building. I hopped along, expecting David Attenborough to pop out at any moment saying, "And here we see a young man with his arse cheeks fused together doing his best impression of a young kangaroo in his natural habitat."

I swung the flat door open and made it to the top of the stairs that led down to the entrance of the building. There was still no sign of anyone left in my building, which I was grateful for given my current problem. I leapt down the steps, taking two at a time with my feet still together. But it was as I reached the last flight of stairs that I suddenly realised that if nobody was left inside with me, they were all outside waiting for me. All eyes were going to be on me so I couldn't go hopping out the door like Skippy in front of everyone, I would be the laughing stock of the building.

I knew I had to walk the rest of the way to save any reputation I had left. The problem was my leg movement was so limited I had to take very small steps. I looked like a speed runner in the Olympics as I waddled my way to the main entrance. I opened the door and, being the last one out, was greeted by not just my flat but everyone in our building. They all stared at me as shuffled over to my flat mates and took up position next to them.

"That took you a while," whispered Layla.

"I know, I was caught in a bit of a sticky situation," I whispered back.

A gentleman in a high-vis jacket stepped to the front of the crowd. "Well done, everyone. That was just a drill, but you all made it out in the expected time … *just* …" he said, glancing over at me.

I hung my head in order to avoid eye contact.

After my little telling off, we were given the usual debrief that we must all ensure we leave the building as soon as possible to avoid injury or death and that next time it might be the real thing.

Shortly after, we were all allowed back inside, but to avoid walking back with everyone and them possibly realising my situation, I made out that I needed to make a phone call.

After pretending to speak to my mum for a couple of minutes, I made my way back inside and hopped my way back up the stairs.

Once back in the flat, I went straight to my room and locked the door behind me. I closed my eyes and wished the whole thing was a dream, but it was very much reality and I still had to find a way of getting the waxing strip off.

I tried to lower myself back down to the original sumo squat position I had taken up earlier, but before I could get anywhere near to the original position the pain became too much. I tried to lower myself again, but this time more slowly, and had a bit more success. Being patient and taking things very slowly, over a period of about twenty minutes, I managed to lower myself right down into the original position I had adopted.

I was back at square one, before the inconvenience of the fire alarm screwed everything up and I took in a deep breath, thankful for the small achievement I had just made. Psyching myself up again, I reached through my legs again and grabbed the rear end of the strip.

I honestly felt exhausted by this point, my legs were aching and I felt mentally drained by the whole ordeal.

"Three ... two ... one ..." I pulled down on the strip, but not hard enough. It had only half come off. Tears filled my eyes with the pain and I bit into my hand to avoid screaming out loud.

After a long bite, I pulled away my hand and saw several teeth marks left on the back of my knuckles. I had bitten down so hard that I had nearly drawn blood. I wiped away the tears that had filled my eyes and blurred my vision. I then steadied myself again before taking another deep breath and grabbing the strip once more. I pulled down with all my might and this time ripped the whole thing off.

I toppled backwards onto my back, breathing sharply in and out as pain spread between my legs. I thought it was going to hurt more than the first pull, but I think the relief of it being detached from my body consumed any pain I had.

I lay on my back and started to laugh. All of that for a hair free bum – something I had never even been bothered by at any point in my life up till now. I heaved myself up and sat upright before picking up the wax strip. Puzzled, I twisted it around and around.

There was no hair visible on it at all?

I looked down at the floor, thinking maybe it came off or something. *How could this be?* I thought to myself.

In panic, I tried to look between my legs, but I couldn't get a good enough view to see what had happened. I ended up making my way over to the bedroom mirror to get a better look. To my horror, I could see that the strips had not actually removed the hair but had in fact stretched them out to considerable length!

"Oh, come on, what the fuck is that?" I shouted without a care in the world if anyone heard.

I continued to stare, mesmerised by the length of the hair now hanging from my arse. It was a sort of pinky colour after mixing with the wax, which meant it now essentially looked as if I had a pink Mohican sticking out of my bum.

I am sure *the girls will love this new look much more than my old one,* I thought to myself.

I stood for a couple more minutes, staring at the pink sonic the hedgehog poking from my rear and thinking what I could do when I had a brainwave.

Maybe all was not lost! I could save the situation and just cut the hair away like a hairdresser.

Feeling confident my new idea would work, I found a pair of scissors in my desk drawer and went to cut the hair off.

Well, the first snip quickly determined that it was, in fact, a terrible idea. I went to cut and immediately the scissors became stuck and entangled in the waxy hair. Stupidly, without thinking, I yanked the scissors in anger to try to free them.

Like before, tears streamed down my face as the most unbelievable, sharp pain shot from where the hairs had pulled at the skin. Never, in nineteen years, had I experienced pain or embarrassment like it.

I stood, looking over my shoulder in the mirror, trying to fathom a way to untangle the scissors properly. I decided rather than pulling them free, I would have to carefully unhook any hairs.

It took me an age to do as the reflection meant everything was back to front. I kept turning left when I meant right, and right when I meant left, but eventually after a long, long time, I was free.

"It's *over*," I said, consoling myself and putting the scissors to one side.

After everything I had been through, I didn't even bother to think about doing any more work down there. I just decided to jump in the shower and washed myself with an entire bottle of shower gel until I had removed virtually all of the wax so it caused me no further problems.

Relieved, I got changed before heading back to the kitchen to find Freddie and Frank sat waiting for me.

They asked how it went and obviously I lied and said it went swimmingly and I was now hair free.

Chapter 9:

I sat in the kitchen by myself, munching on some cereal and trying to forget the pain I experienced the night before. I couldn't get it out of my head and was struggling to get comfortable. Shuffling about on the plastic kitchen chairs I realised that, after being at uni for a while now, I really missed a lot of the little things from back home. A comfy chair, a sofa – a beanbag, even. I mean, the halls I lived in were not bad, but you really did miss some of the home comforts.

I fidgeted about, trying to adjust myself into a better position on my chair when the kitchen door opened and Freddie walked in.

"How you doing, man?" he asked.

"Yeah, not too bad, thanks, just trying to knuckle down and get some work done," I said.

Freddie explained he was in the same boat. Work was beginning to pile up and although we still had quite a bit of time left, the thought of summer exams was becoming more and more of a concern to us all.

The problem I had was that whenever I tried to get going, I got distracted or I procrastinated. I would do anything to avoid actually doing work.

It even came to the point that I was tidying my room to the highest degree of cleanliness – I was *that* determined to avoid revision.

Instead of getting on and writing up more revision cards than I usually would, I found myself doing the slowest clean up in history and once that killed two hours, I then went to find my flatmates to be a bad influence on them.

I looked to see if anything was going on at uni to attend that didn't involve work. Today there was a karaoke competition going on down at the SU. I didn't sing, nor had I ever tried karaoke, but, hey, if it meant me avoiding the module on EU law then it was good enough for me.

I managed to persuade Layla to come join me and before long we were sat down at the local SU bar listening to someone who thought they were far better at singing than they actually were attempt "Angels" by Robbie Williams. This is, or should I say *had* been, one of my favourite songs, but dear old Fred's version ruined it forever for me.

I sat on the table and covered my ears as Fred tried to hit a high note. A horrible squeal, much like that of a dog having his tail stepped on, passed by his lips and he stopped himself from completing the song much to the relief of us all in the audience.

The applause he received was more out of pity than anything else.

Layla and I had to hold back our sniggers as the organiser thanked Fred for his efforts. I chuckled to myself as I imagined Layla or I giving it a go up on stage.

"Next up, Luke Fagg with 'I Believe In a Thing Called Love' by The Darkness."

I snapped my head around to the stage, thinking I must have misheard what had been said.

Silence fell across the room as people looked about for me.

How had this happened, I hadn't volunteered?

The laughter from Layla soon answered my question.

I cursed at her as she pointed me out to the host. He urged me to come on up, but I shook my head. Unfortunately, he was one of those people who had too much enthusiasm (you know the ones) and wouldn't take no for an answer. He got the rest of audience involved and people began clapping slowly and chanting my name in order to encourage me. Layla pushed me up from my chair and there was a roar as I was forced to my feet.

There was no way I could sit back down now.

Embarrassed by the whole situation, I timidly made my way to the stage where I was told the lyrics would appear on the screen in front of me. If you have not heard of the song I performed, please would you take a moment to look it up and just appreciate just how hard it is to sing – impossible, even.

Knowing that the song has a very high-pitched tone throughout, with a particular note far higher than the others, I started in as low a voice as possible. As I began, I was cheered and shouted words of encouragement, which I have to say helped boost my confidence.

As the song got going, I actually began to get into it and felt a sense of confidence growing. Don't get me wrong, I'm not saying I had suddenly turned into Adele, but I was passable at least.

I kept going, knowing the high pitch note was getting ever closer and I could tell the anticipation was growing from the crowd, too.

The line arrived on the screen in front of me and I went for it.

Stupidly, I went for it.

It was if I hit puberty for a second time as my voice broke *and* squeaked at the same time.

The collective intake of breath from every person watching made it clear it wasn't a good noise and I ended up finishing the rest of the song with my tail very much between my legs and a face as red as a tomato.

As I hit the final note of the song, I actually got a resounding cheer.

It was a lot better than the reaction for Fred's performance so that's all that mattered. They knew I had been stitched up by Layla, but they seemed to appreciate I gave it a go at least and had been a good sport about it.

I made my way back to the table where Layla was in hysterics. I took a theatrical bow in front of her and laughed as I rose to see her continue to giggle away to herself. She presented me with a pint, as in fact did the organiser shortly after, to say well done for taking part.

With little to eat and a few drinks down me, I was a little tipsy and I said to Layla maybe it was best we head home before things got too out of hand.

Arriving back at the flat, we found things actually *had* got out of hand. It was a Friday and with no lectures tomorrow, it was not just myself and Layla who had been drinking. Everyone else in the flat had started too and we walked in on them playing an innocent game of truth or dare in the kitchen.

The second we entered, Anna was quick to tell us that Freddie had just admitted to having a threesome. I was shocked, as was Layla.

It turned out it was when he was seventeen with two girls from his college who both asked him if he would be up for it.

After querying him further, we asked the others what truth or dares they had done. Frank had already drunk a tablespoon of soy sauce and Anna had eaten an entire onion, apparently taking fifteen minutes to do so!

With more drink being consumed, the game soon became more and more outrageous. I was up next and I chose dare. The others took some time to think carefully about what I could do and after a while decided that I should run around our halls of residence in my just my boxers.

With quite a substantial amount of alcohol now pumping its way through my veins, I was well up for the task – in fact, I had virtually all my clothes off before they had even finished explaining what I had to do.

The reason why I was so full of confidence was not just the alcohol, but also the fact that I knew a lot of people went home on Friday nights so there was likely to be hardly anyone on campus. I was expecting a pretty clear and easy four hundred metre sprint.

With all my clothes – except my boxers – eventually removed, I shuffled off downstairs to the main hall entrance.

I checked out the window to see how things were looking outside and, to my joy, there was nobody about. I clicked open the door and immediately broke into a sprint. It wasn't long before I was flying, but quickly the rough ground scraping at my feet meant I had to slow up.

I swung a right towards the bus station and was expecting there to be nobody there, but to my horror there was and it wasn't just one person but a whole team.

To be exact, it was the rugby team.

I stopped in my tracks as the group looked me up and down with their kit bags hung over their broad, muscular shoulders. I thought I could just play off my current clothing attire and they would laugh when I explained the situation, but before I could open my mouth to explain, a familiar figure stepped forward from the group.

It was Andy and, by the look in his face, he wasn't going to listen to anything I had to say. He just wanted to cause me some pain.

I took one step back to head the way I had come, but Andy copied my move. He then shouted at the others that I was the guy from that incident at the start of the year.

On hearing this, the others immediately took a step forward, too. He must have told them what happened and now they were going to back him up. Still tip toeing backwards, I tried to reason with the guys and explained it was all part of a game and could we not forget the start of the year, seeing as it was a long time ago?

The fact that they started sprinting at me soon confirmed that was a no and there was no chance of negotiating.

I turned on a six pence and made off as quickly as I could. They were already close behind me so I knew there was no chance I could get back through the main door to my halls now. It would take too long to open and they would be on me before I could get inside. Instead, I would have to build a lead and use that to give me enough time to get back inside unharmed.

I used to run a lot with my dad when I was younger and so I was confident in my ability to outpace the rugby yobs, especially as they were a lot larger than I was. With my plan set out in my head, I picked up the pace and began to open up a gap. A quick check over my shoulder and I could see I was about ten metres ahead and the gap was widening with each stride I took. I looked ahead towards the corner I would have to take next when I noticed a reflection shine off the surface of the ground just ahead of me. I squinted, trying to see what it could be as I got closer and the pain in my feet soon confirmed my worst fear.

It was glass.

I trod down on a piece with my left foot and felt a small, jagged shard cut the sole of my foot. I cursed at the pain while I hopped a couple of times, shaking my leg to try to get the piece out of my foot. Thankfully, it worked, but now the gap was down to just five metres.

Sensing they were gaining, the group began taunting me, however, as their voices lessened in volume, I knew I must have been gaining a bigger lead again.

I got to the corner of the building and swung myself round hard, brushing my hand against the bricks as I did so. Shortly after, I was around the next corner and heading down the back straight of the building. I could see the far end about one hundred and fifty metres away and knew two more corners with the lead I had could easily mean I got inside unhurt.

I tore off now at maximum speed with hope and a sense of liberation filling my body.

This was short lived, however, as to my horror, I saw a figure turn the corner at the far end ahead of me. Even though they were far away, I could make out straight away that it was Andy.

He must have decided to cut me off.

I had the halls to my left and a tall brick wall to my right. With the path I was running along being so narrow, there was very little room for me to squeeze past Andy – in fact, given his size, there was virtually none.

I looked around desperately for another means of escape. I thought about climbing the wall, but it was just too high. There was no way I could get a hand over the top to grip it. The halls, though? Could there be an emergency exit? No, but there were windows and I spotted one that had been left wide open about seventy-five metres ahead.

I knew that to get in and have time to close it, I would essentially have to dive through the window headfirst.

I adjusted my angle of approach and, just as Andy was about fifteen metres away and the others behind me a similar distance, I dived through the gap.

On landing, I slammed into a chest of drawers before immediately spinning round and thumping the window shut and locking it. Seconds later, my pursuers were banging on the window, shouting at me and calling me every name under the sun.

Knowing I was safe, I cheekily waved at them as I closed the curtains to vanish them from my view. The banging continued for a bit longer before they gave up, knowing they had no chance of getting to me now.

Relieved, I turned, completely forgetting I had just dived through some random person's window.

It was as I was spinning around that I got a real shock; I saw a lad my age sat on his bed dressed in all sorts of bondage gear, including a gag ball in his mouth.

I froze as we stared at one another. What the hell had I walked into?

We stared it out for what must have been at least ten seconds, but it was broken as a sound from his laptop broke my concentration. I looked over to his computer screen, where a message had popped up saying a new viewer has just paid £5 for five-minute private show. That is when it twigged with me that this bloke must be some kind of online fetish sex worker.

I looked from the laptop back to him and he nodded towards the door, gesturing for me to leave. I knew that people had to make a living to get through uni and this was something I had heard about before. Trying to keep out of shot of his web cam and to keep his new paying customer happy, I crawled along the floor to the bedroom door.

I stood up to let myself out and as I did so, I heard a mumble behind me.

The guy was giving me a thumbs up and then winked as I gave one back. Well, I strangely felt rather good for having helped out this bloke. I had not disturbed whatever show he was performing at that point (that much) and hopefully he'd get some good reviews because of it!

Out in the corridor, the realisation that I had been chased by Andy and his mates suddenly hit me.

What if they had got hold of me? Would they have beaten me up or stripped me naked to humiliate me? Trying to block horrible thoughts out of my head, I picked up a jog to this stranger's front door and then began to climb the stairs back to safety. My feat felt heavy and drained as my bare soles rubbed against the vinyl flooring.

I arrived at my floor and Freddie was already stood there with the door open and shepherded me in.

Slightly out of breath, I sat down and slumped myself against the wall. I didn't say anything as I tried to think about what had just happened when Layla pointed out the state of my feet. With all the adrenaline, my body must have just forgotten about all the pain, but looking down my entire left foot was caked in blood. It actually looked as if it had been dip dyed in some red paint!

Layla headed to the kitchen and was quick to come back with a cloth and water. Without asking, she started to clean my wound.

I winced as the hot water entered the cut, but Layla continued to gently wipe away the dirt and soon my foot was clean.

Anna came back with some bandages shortly after and wrapped them round so the foot was fully protected from infection or anything else nasty. They then sat with me in the corridor and explained they had seen it all unfold from their bedroom windows.

They told me that Andy's mates had been saying they were going to beat the shit out of me.

Apparently, Anna was just about to ring the university security, but stopped herself when she saw me jump through the window downstairs. They asked if anyone was in the room and, naturally, I lied and told them there wasn't – I didn't really feel like telling them I had walked into a Fifty Shades of Grey parody.

We sat in silence for about thirty seconds, which was eventually broken by Layla jokingly asking if anyone fancied another round of truth or dare.

Chapter 10:

A few more weeks passed by at university and nothing of real significance happened. With coursework needing to be handed in and people starting to stress more and more about exams, we were all in our own little worlds as we studied away in the library or took more time out to cram some revision in, rather than getting up to our usual mischief.

However, today was going to be different because today was my birthday! It had fallen on a Saturday, which was perfect as it meant my flatmates and I could all go out to celebrate it without the worry of lectures the next day and I had been told that they all had a surprise for me. Waking nice and early, I made my way to the kitchen where I was greeted with balloons and cheers from them all.

I was given hugs and handed a shot of tequila. It was 10:00, but I had been told that I had to start the day as I intended to go on. Throwing it down my neck, I winced at the taste – I should have had the flavour of peppermint mouthwash filling my taste buds, not alcohol!

I was then told I had to get dressed and be ready for a sit down meal at a local pub for noon. I was shocked, these lovely housemates –

despite being students and not having a lot of money – had all chipped in to pay for a meal and drinks for me. I was touched and thanked them all for their kindness. I honestly was not expecting it at all.

With a bit of time to kill before heading off, I phoned my parents and sister and also replied to the birthday messages I had been sent from my friends back home. I was really happy to receive so many and it put me in a really good mood going into the day. Like a kid at Christmas, I cheerily got showered and changed.

Seeing as the guys had made such an effort with things, I thought I should too and dressed in a smart shirt and chinos.

Arriving back at the kitchen, I was surprised to see that Layla was the only one ready. She was wearing a flowing blue top and tight jeans and she had also curled the ends of her hair. She looked amazing and I found myself smiling before I had even sat down next to her. When I asked where the others were, she just said she didn't know and asked if we could get a picture together. I happily agreed and she wrapped her arm around me for the selfie.

A short time later, the others arrived and Anna said she liked the picture of us two. I was confused at how Anna had seen it so she took out her phone and showed me the picture of Layla and I that had been posted on Facebook. I was quite amazed at the amount of likes and comments it already had and was pleased at how happy we both looked in the photo.

With everyone ready, I was led by the others on a walk to the local pub. It was a short walk away and the traditional wooden exterior of the building contrasted the more modern interior finish. It was very much a "young person's" pub – cheap drink and food, but it still had quality in abundance.

Once sat down, we ordered a round of drinks and then decided on our mains. I went for the "Mighty" burger, an enormous beef burger with every filling you could imagine partnered with double cooked chips and a dollop of garlic mayo on the side.

I was simply in heaven.

I gorged on my food as did the others until our plates were squeaky clean. We ordered another round of drinks but, before they arrived, I excused myself to the toilet.

I was about to break the seal with my first bathroom trip of the day.

Freddie decided he needed to break the seal too and he followed me in to the men's, leaving the others and their food babies at the table. At the urinals, I thanked Freddie again for helping sort the meal, but he insisted it was mainly down to Layla and there was only one thing he had really been put in charge of.

When I asked what that was, he produced a small packet from his pocket that contained two pink pills. I instantly knew they were drugs, but had no idea what type.

"Ecstasy," said Freddie.

"Mate. I have never even smoked weed, let alone done a pill before," I explained.

Freddie held out his hand and stopped me. Firstly, he explained there was no pressure for me to take anything. He had seen some of his friends forced into doing them before and said it was not nice to see. Secondly, he said if I were to take it, he would regulate it and only give me a maximum of a third of a pill at a time as he did not want me losing my shit straight away.

Feeling happy I had a choice, I, maybe surprisingly, declined the offer. I just didn't want to risk it. I had heard too many stories of people having bad reactions to them or becoming addicted straight away.

Hearing this and without a fuss, Freddie said he totally understood and then we made our way back to the table.

We finished off our meals before I was told it was time to move on to the next pub. This was going to be a pub crawl before we ended up in a club. With stomachs filled with food, we all headed down the next stop about half a mile away. A quick pint and we were on to the next.

As the day went on, and as we caught the football at a couple of the pubs, we began to slow. We were becoming drunk and our bodies were not handling the alcohol as well as they were at the start.

We sensibly decided to ease off as we knew anymore could spurn our chances of being let into the club later. Instead of drinking, we just sat and chatted. No phones, no games, we just chatted.

It is amazing what conversations alcohol can bring out in people and it wasn't long before we got on the topic of a zombie apocalypse.

Well, this particular conversation must have gone on for about an hour. Honestly, the detail we got into was quite alarming, really. Do you stake it out and stay put and hope help comes your way or do you head out for supplies? I bet you're thinking about it in your head right now.

I personally said that the best plan would be to head to an outer suburb of London, find a small shop and stock up on supplies as best you could before trying to communicate with friends or family. The others disagreed, saying everyone would have the same idea to find supplies and would get there before me and that they would then shoot me or wound me if I entered the shop! Honestly, the possibilities and scenarios that kept coming up were endless and there was virtually no plan that we could all agree was watertight.

After this long conversation, we sobered up slightly – don't get me wrong, we were still drunk, but we were just the right side of the limit to be let into the club and so that's where we headed next.

When we arrived, we were virtually the first ones in as the night was still young. With time to kill, we decided to grab a booth by the dancefloor and have a few more drinks.

Being as early as we were, we actually arrived at happy hour and we took full advantage of the buy one, get one free offer by grabbing four double vodka lemonades each.

As we sat in the booth sipping at our drinks, the club quickly filled up and it was not long before the atmosphere really picked up.

With the music booming and the dancefloor filling, Freddie gave me a nudge and said he was popping off to the toilet. I could see from his face that he meant he was going to drop a pill while he was in there too.

A couple of minutes later, he came back. He was very chilled and was holding a pack of gum he had bought off the toilet attendant. He sat back down next to us and pooped a chewing gum in his mouth before quickly pointing out how drunk Anna had suddenly become. Layla and I had not noticed as we were too engaged in our own conversation, but Anna's eyes were virtually shut and she was beginning to slump over. We shook her to wake her up a bit, but she came round for all of thirty seconds before slumping back in her seat again.

I laughed and said that we best get her home but the others insisted that it should not ruin my night and to get out on the dancefloor. I understood where they were coming from, but I thought it wrong to leave Anna by herself. We ended up agreeing we would take turns babysitting. Layla volunteered the first shift and so Freddie and I headed out to throw some terrible, drunken moves.

Everyone on the dancefloor must have ended up knowing it was my birthday with the way Freddie was telling every Tom, Dick and Harry who was passing by. But the truth was, and rather vainly of me, I actually quite enjoyed the attention it was bringing to me.

After about thirty minutes, Freddie said he would go swap with Layla and so I watched as he hurried off before seeing Layla make her way onto the dancefloor.

Before anything was even said, she took me by the hand and span me round. She laughed as I nearly lost my balance and then proceeded to spin me the other way. Again, I nearly lost my balance and in revenge, I decided to return the favour. To my amazement, Layla span round with ease and when I tried to catch her out again she just took it in her stride.

We carried on dancing and laughing at my awful dance moves before I got a glimpse over her shoulder at Freddie and Anna. It was clear that the ecstasy had really kicked in and it made for one of the most bizarre and hilarious things I had ever seen.

Freddie was now stood up and shuffling away like he was stood on hot coals. His feet were a complete blur and his jaw was gurning away like there was no tomorrow. The thing that made it bizarre was that he was still trying to look after Anna and so his right arm was stroking her frantically, like an overly keen child stroking a cat. This was all whilst Anna lay like a rag doll across the seats – they were the two total opposite ends of the spectrum!

I stood for a moment to admire Freddie's efforts. Despite his best impression of Footloose, which caused his body to move all over the place, he still had the caring side of him as he tried his best to direct his ever-wandering hands on to Anna's back. It was a sight to behold. However, I was not the only who had seen it. Out of the corner of my eye, I could see a bouncer making his way over to the booth.

I grabbed Layla and said I thought we best sort things out before the others got in trouble.

We arrived just before the bouncer got to them.

"Come on, guys, we need to get home now, you've had too much," I said loudly enough that the bouncer could hear.

I put an arm under Anna and Layla got the other side to support her. I pulled her up from the chair and she moaned as we dragged her to her feet. The bouncer came over to check for sure we were leaving and I assured him we were.

As much as Freddie wanted to help, we thought it best to leave him out of it because we feared he may get in the way more than helping. With Anna cradled between us, myself and Layla dragged her along the floor past the bar and outside through the exit.

At the taxi rank, it was not surprising that nobody would take us. We had a Strictly Come Dancing wannabe and a girl who looked as if she was on the verge of death. Giving ourselves time to think, we propped Anna on a bench and considered options available.

All the buses had stopped running as it was so late and with no taxis willing to take us there was really only one option left and that was to walk. It was only just over a mile but with Anna in the state she was, we knew it was more of a challenge than it sounded.

As you can imagine, though, Freddie was well up for it.

He was still two-stepping from side to side and, had he been wearing a Fit Bit, I am sure he would have hit a new record with his step count with all the movement going on.

Looking at one another, Layla and I got a hold of Anna, as we had done back at the club, and began to walk. Freddie led the way and gleefully ran ahead for us to check whether there were benches en route for us to stop and take a break whenever Anna became a bit too heavy.

We must have stopped around four times in the end before arriving back at the flat. Freddie held all of the doors open and after eventually finding Anna's bedroom key in her jeans pocket, we laid her down on the bed to sleep on her side, worried about her rolling on her back and throwing up – the last thing we wanted was for her to choke on her own vomit in the night.

Freddie, being in the mood he was, offered to look after Anna but we kindly rejected that, pointing out he was likely to wake the downstairs neighbours with the Irish jig he kept performing. Instead, Layla and I decided to take it in shifts.

I would do the first two hours and then wake Layla and she would take over. We would then keep switching until it was morning or we knew Anna would be okay.

I propped myself up against the door of Anna's room while Layla found a pillow to lie on. I wished her a good night and then took out my phone to try to find something on Facebook or YouTube to keep myself entertained for my shift. I ended up in the world of crazy videos of YouTube. You know, the ones where you just click related video after related video and then all of a sudden find a thirty-minute video called, *Ten Ocean Mysteries That Have Never Been Solved* and think, oh, go on then.

With my knowledge of ocean mysteries and unsolved crimes now significantly widened and the two hours up, I had to wake Layla. I felt terrible about doing it and after the first attempt of waking her failing, the second was even harder to do as I could see how much of a deep sleep she was in and how peaceful she was.

Eventually, she stirred awake and I immediately apologised for having woken her. Although we had agreed on it, I still felt bad having done so. However, with a small smile across her face, she insisted it was okay and after similarly taking out her phone – but ignoring my suggestion of unsolved mysteries – she started her two hours watching some videos.

I woke the next morning on the floor with the light through the crack in the curtains shining in my face. I clicked my phone on next to me and read the time. 08:00. What? No! I had swapped with Layla at 04:00, she should have woken me ages ago.

She must have fallen asleep.

Did that mean Anna had been left without anyone checking on her?

I span around to check on Anna and Layla. There, sat quietly, still watching videos on her phone, was Layla and, next to her, Anna still sound asleep.

I pushed myself off my pillow and then realised I had a blanket covering me as it slid off my upper body. I quickly asked Layla why she didn't wake me, I felt terrible.

She just explained that I looked too peaceful and so she didn't bother and instead got a blanket from her room to keep me warm.

I smiled at her. I didn't have to say thank you because she could see from the look on my face just how grateful I was.

I couldn't help myself and dropped the cliché, "Any guy would be lucky to have you."

As cringey as it was, she blushed and tried to laugh it off.

"I think I am going to be sick," moaned Anna, waking up.

"You still feeling ill, then, Anna?" I asked.

"Well, I wasn't till I heard that awful, cheesy line," she laughed.

Layla and I both joined in before handing Anna a glass of water. It was clear she was in a bad way and she quickly wrote off the day, saying she was only going to sleep and watch Disney movies for the next twenty-four hours.

Leaving her to it, Layla and I made our way back to our rooms.

Taking a similar approach to Anna, I also essentially took Sunday off too and decided on sleeping and catching the football through the day. I even took the lazy approach of having food delivered in to my flat I was in such a 'can't be bothered' mood.

But, despite having such a laid-back day, I did take the opportunity to look on the university website for any extra revision classes. With exams approaching, I needed to take any opportunity I could to get in some extra work. Scrolling through, I found that there were classes running all week for each module of our course and I noted down the rooms and time on a piece of paper so I would be able to attend them.

Feeling pretty chuffed with myself at having written down about twenty words, I decided on calling it a day with work and went back to watching to see whether my beloved football team Fulham FC could get a much-needed win.

Chapter 11:

I woke on Monday at 07:00 and felt full of energy. After a shower and a good breakfast, I made my way to a lecture hall for the first revision session of the week I had written down. I arrived fifteen minutes before the lesson started and so found myself to be the only one there. I was keen to get a good view of the whiteboard and PowerPoint slides that no doubt would appear on the wall from the overhead projector and so I sat myself bang in the middle of the front row.

I took out my pen and a pad of paper as well as my book on EU Law, which I gave a little read as I waited for everyone else to arrive. I only managed about two pages before nearly every seat in the room was taken. Looking around, I couldn't really recognise anyone, but then again when it comes to exams, everyone starts attending seminars even if they didn't make it to any lectures throughout the early part of the year, so it wasn't a surprise to me.

Five minutes before the lesson started, our lecturer walked in. He greeted us all and then started up his laptop. There was a silence across the room as we eagerly awaited for the PowerPoint to show up. We did not know what he was going to cover, but I was hoping it was going to be on the free movement of goods within the EU; it was not a strong topic of mine so any more information on it would help me.

The projection slowly came to life.

The Stages of Pregnancy filled the wall in front of us all.

I laughed, thinking it must be some kind of joke but nobody else joined in. Instead, they all wrote down the title at the top of their page.

I uneasily looked around me when suddenly the lecturer spoke, "As you may have guessed from the title, we are going to be reviewing pregnancy, one of the main topics that will come up in the exams for your degree."

What degree? I thought to myself.

I looked around at the people sat either side of me.

Each of them had a book on midwifery. I was in the wrong bloody lecture. Here I was, sat with a book on how goods are shipped from one EU country to another, and next to me I had a girl with a book on how a baby ends up popping out of a woman.

Not only had I got the wrong lecture, but with my eagerness to get a good seat for what was now a totally useless lesson, I had approximately fifteen people sat either side of me. This meant if I made a move to leave, I would have to ask them all to stand up in front of everyone so I could do the Space Invader sideways walk of shame to make my way to the exit. The thought of doing this was too embarrassing for me and so I stupidly decided to stay. I mean, it was only a revision session so I would not expect it to be that long anyway.

Without anyone noticing, I packed my EU law book back into my bag and decided to make notes. That's right, I actually started taking bloody notes in this lecture that had nothing to do with my degree. An hour passed – a painstaking hour, I should point out – and the lecturer was still in full flow.

Thirty minutes later, I was grateful to hear that we were nearly at the end.

With ten minutes to go, the lecturer stopped the PowerPoint and took out a piece of paper from his blue folder. He then explained on it were a list of questions and he would be picking people out to answer them.

A pop quiz, essentially.

Stepping forward, the lecturer started, "This is an easy one to begin with. A multipara whose ultrasound suggests a foetus of 3200 g progresses in labour then remains at six cm dilatation for three hours. Foetal heart rate tracing is reactive. An intrauterine pressure catheter reveals two contractions in ten minutes with an amplitude of forty mm Hg each. What would be the best management for this patient?"

Well, my mum is a nurse but, perhaps unsurprisingly, I had never asked her this particular question and so didn't have a fucking clue.

With the class silent, the teacher lifted a finger and pointed at – yep, you guessed it – he pointed at me.

I sat stock still as I felt every set of eyes in the room lock on to me.

Think, Luke, think! Anything just half decent would at least not blow my cover.

The awkward silence grew in the room as I racked my brain.

"I'll have to push you as we are running out on time," said the lecturer.

"Errmm … I would recommend that you …" I stumbled. I just couldn't get any words out. I had nothing to offer.

In a panic, and in a desperate bid to escape, I just grabbed my bag from beneath me, got out of my seat and hopped over the long desk in front of me.

The lecturer took a step back in shock as I stood in front of him and the rest of the class.

In an attempt to show I meant no harm, I bowed towards him with my hands by my side without saying a word. Then, I simply made my way to the exit in the most awkward silence you could imagine.

As the door closed behind me, I could hear the roar of laughter and, to be honest, I couldn't blame them. I mean, they had just witnessed a bloke crumble under the pressure of what is considered an easy question and then jump out of his seat before performing a bow like some kind of Judo fighter who had just lost to his opponent.

It's fair to say that I didn't really hang around for long.

I was not very keen on being caught by any people who may have been in there and might ask me what the hell I was doing.

Instead, I made a quick getaway down the nearest set of stairs and took out the piece of paper I had written down the rooms on the night before. Room N1010 was in blue ink in front of me. I looked back to where I had come from and saw a sign above the hall entrance reading N1001.

What an idiot, I thought to myself.

I quickly looked down the rest of the list and saw that there was another revision session starting in an hour's time not far away. Feeling a little miffed at having missed out on one already, I decided to pop to the library to do some revision by myself before the next one started.

I really needed to make full use of my time.

Chapter 12:

The next couple of months flew by and, when I say flew by, I mean at an incredibly alarming rate. Exams were starting in a week and we had been given the full breakdown of how they would work.

It was simple, we had three sectors of law we had studied that year. In each of those sectors there were thirteen modules, but in the exam there would only be six modules given to us. Of these six, you only have to answer two. Still with me? Well, with a potential thirteen modules and with six coming up, it essentially meant you had to learn seven modules in a good amount of detail to guarantee you could answer at least two questions.

It was when I was sat in the library with some of my course mates that I realised the seriousness of the situation.

Many of the questions were scenarios and while everyone else was able to answer them with ease, I couldn't. Every past paper question we went through I missed a key element that meant I would get maximum a 2:2. I wanted a 2:1 as a minimum and so I had to think of a strategy.

The truth was, I did not have enough time to revise all seven topics in enough depth to bring that 2:2 or 3rd up to a 2:1. My brain simply would not be able to take it. Instead, I was going to have to gamble – but it was going to be an educated gamble.

I took all of the past papers from the last five years for each sector and made a tally chart of what had come up previously.

My course mates were baffled as I trawled through each one, but eventually I had two clear leaders for two of the sectors and then three tied for the last.

Realising what I was up to, Tom, who was on my course, stopped me and said what I was going to do was madness.

He was right, it was utter madness but I really had no other choice. In my eyes, I would seriously rather retake the year (which I have done before at A-level, remember) than walk out with a 2:2 or 3rd. If I wanted to make it into a law firm, I needed to get the high marks they were going to want.

Tom pointed out they probably wanted people with a broad knowledge of all the sectors rather than two parts, but that wasn't important to me at the time.

Looking at my list, I had gone from a total of twenty-one topics to revise to just five. I was quite chuffed with myself, but the others pointed out that if one or, in the worst case, two didn't come up, I would fail.

But it was a risk I was willing to take. I know you probably think I'm mad.

With a week to go, I decided on revising one topic a day and on the last day have a big catch up, reading through them all. With the others in utter shock as to what they had just heard, I started and over the next week I revised every day in as much depth as possible. I would read my notes with breakfast, lunch and dinner and I also did not drink a single drop of alcohol throughout the seven days in order for my brain to be in top gear.

With all the revision I was doing, it came to the night before my exam and although I had studied a huge amount on the topics of my choice, there was still that niggling thought in the back of my brain that I may have studied all the wrong topics and that none of them would actually come up at all ...

Trying to keep my mind off this, I decided to relax a bit by watching a film before I went to bed.

It was halfway through the film that I realised I had taken none of what had happened on screen into my head. I just kept playing the same scenario of opening the question book tomorrow and there not being the questions I wanted over and over in my head. In an attempt to get my mind off it, I decided to play some online games instead. They were more engaging than a film and so would get my brain thinking more and away from the thoughts of failure.

Six games and six losses of eight-ball pool later and I realised it was no use. I was caught in a terrible whirlwind of negative thoughts and could not escape it. Instead of fighting it any more, I just decided the best thing was to head to bed. It was about 22:00 anyway so it was best I got as much rest as possible because it was a 09:00 start for my first exam the next day.

Resting my head on my pillow, I tried to drift off ...

Five hours later, I was still trying to drift off. It was 02:00! My exam was in seven hours and I needed my sleep! I started playing that stupid game in my head: *well, if I get to sleep now, I will get X hours sleep still*.

The problem was that the hours were just getting smaller and smaller and smaller. I closed my eyes and tried to drift off once more.

Beep. Beep. Beep. My alarm was sounding and there was also a banging at my door. What was going on?

"Luke! Luke, wake up!" shouted a voice. It was Layla.

I looked at the time on my alarm clock. It was 08:45. I had overslept.

I opened up my door to find Layla looking just as worried as I was. She shouted at me to get ready. I was just in my boxers and I fumbled around in my wardrobe to find anything I could quickly slip on to make it out as quickly as possible.

Layla stood at the door and asked me if I needed anything and if she could help. I asked her for a couple of pens as I wrestled to get my trousers on.

I grabbed my student ID from my drawer and pulled on a t-shirt before glancing at the time. I had thirteen minutes to get across to the exam. Well, you might remember that it only takes me ten minutes to run to my law lecture hall, so I knew I should be able to make it in time, however, my exam was not in the lecture hall – It was in the main exam hall on the other campus, which is a ten minute bus ride away.

To put it bluntly, I was terrified.

A whole year could be ruined because I overslept.

I sprinted out into the corridor. Layla was stood outside her room holding two pens.

I didn't even have time to stop and say goodbye properly, I just sprinted past, grabbing them and shouting my thanks to her over my shoulder. Bursting through the front door, I swung onto the stairs and took three at a time in an attempt to save as much time as I could.

Hurtling out of the front door like a greyhound fuelled on cocaine, I bounded around the corner and headed towards the bus stop.

There was nobody stood there and with sudden, horrible realisation I could see why.

The bus was up the road and turning the corner, heading to the other campus.

I cursed and began to panic. I looked up at the timetable on the screen. The next one was in five minutes. It was no good to me as it would never arrive to the other campus on time.

What could I do?

Just as I was about to start tearing off down the road in an attempt to run to the other campus, I saw a taxi down the road from me. It was for hire and heading my way. Waving my arms and screaming like a lost soul who was stuck on an island and had just seen a passing ship after five years of being stranded, I ran towards the taxi, hailing it down. A flash of its lights let me know the driver had seen me as I sprinted towards him. A sudden happiness surged over my body as I thought I would actually make the exam.

Unfortunately, in my haste to get in the taxi as quickly as possible, I took my eyes off the pavement I was running along and the tip of my shoe caught the edge of an uneven slab. If it weren't for the speed I was travelling at, I am sure I would have kept my balance, but with my legs pumping as hard as they were, the slightest of touches sent me tumbling to the floor.

I stuck out my arms as best I could to act as a breaker for my fall and pain shot up my forearm as I came crashing down on the concrete. With so little time, I didn't even check to see how badly cut I was, I just leapt back to my feet and hopped my way to the passenger door with my big toe throbbing.

I went to open the door but it was locked.

I watched as the window slowly wound down and the bloke asked me where I was heading.

I quickly explained the situation and that I needed to be on the other campus within the next five minutes or else the chances were I failed the year. On hearing everything, the guy very calmly just told me to hop in.

I threw myself into the car and slammed the door behind me.

"Excuse me, sir, would you treat your own car in that manner?" asked the driver.

"I'm sorry, mate, I just really need to get to this lecture!" I pleaded.

"Well, I suggest you change your attitude or that's not going to happen," he replied.

I apologised and expected him to start driving but instead he nodded towards the door.

I couldn't believe it, he was telling me to get out!

I begged him not to kick me out, offering him twenty quid for what was a five-minute journey to make up for slamming his door.

He then explained he wasn't actually kicking me out, he just wanted me to get out and get back in the car in a more polite and gentle manner. I couldn't believe what I was hearing. Here I was, desperate to make it to an exam and I was getting a bloody talking to from this guy like he was my mum!

With no time to argue, I quickly unclipped my belt and got out of the car. I very carefully shut the door behind me and heard the doors lock. I stood there, expecting the worse and for him to drive off after tricking me, but instead he just wound down the window again and asked me where I was going.

I stood there perplexed.

"I just told you!" I cried, baffled.

"Where are you heading to, sir?"

"The other campus for my exam, please!"

"Very well. Please hop in."

I quickly grabbed the handle and got into the passenger's seat again before very carefully shutting the door behind me.

"See, much better." The driver smiled.

I smiled back but the truth was I wanted to scream. Was this guy just taking the piss?

I bet he drives like a bloody granny, too, I thought to myself.

I clicked my seatbelt on and all of a sudden the car lurched forward as the taxi man slammed on the accelerator. Before I knew it, we were already at the end of the road and with only the slightest dab on the brakes, we flew around the roundabout and off towards the other campus.

I gripped the passenger door handle as we careered down the road at twice the speed limit. Ahead of us was a long straight with rows of speed bumps. Ignoring all signs to slow down, the driver sent us bumping over the first so hard my arse actually left the seat. For a man so precious about his doors, he clearly did not give a toss about the rest of his car. We smashed into another as we gained on a car in front.

I looked up, expecting us to slow and fall in behind the silver BMW now blocking our path but, to my horror, the taxi swung out to the other side of the road and was looking to overtake. I could see a bus coming the other way and, thinking my life was about to end, I curled myself into a ball and looked away from the several tonnes of metal now heading our way. I closed my eyes and heard the sound of a car horn as our car weaved back to the correct side of the road.

With no crash *or* signs of our car stopping, I slowly opened my eyes to the sound of laughter coming from my driver.

He was hysterical, bragging about how close we had come to hitting the bus.

In light of what just happened, I politely asked him if he was fucking mental.

Another bellow of laughter quickly confirmed to me that he was.

We were still flying and after a few more turns I took a quick look at the clock on the dashboard, which confirmed I still had four minutes till my exam. I gripped the dashboard in front of me as we went over the last speedbump and with the screech of tyres, we arrived at the other campus.

Fearing for my life, but also wanting to make my exam, I just threw £20 at my maniac of a driver and bolted out of the door.

With pen and student ID still in hand, I ran through the car park and to the exam building.

I could see an exam invigilator stood by the front door and he was holding it open. I shouted at him to keep it open as I sprinted towards him.

Despite noticing me and to my utter disbelief, the man tapped his watch and began to swing around the heavy door.

I was absolutely furious.

He had seen me and yet was taking it upon himself to ruin my chances of getting a degree – what a bloody low life! Well, I had not come this far to give up and so continued heading straight for the door.

Just as it was about to close, I hit it at full tilt.

The door flew open and sent the invigilator flying across the exam hall floor. The noise echoed around the room as he let out a scream.

I stood there as three hundred pairs of eyes all stared at me.

"Sorry I'm late," I said to fill the silence. "Traffic was a nightmare."

You could hear a pin drop as I went over to help up the gentleman I had just sent flying. As I brought him to his feet, I was quick to point out that had it been his son running for the door, I was sure he would have kept it open.

I must have looked very intimidating as the guy nodded frankly, agreeing he was in the wrong.

Giving him a firm pat on the back, I scanned the room to see where I should be sat.

There was one table and chair free in the entire hall and so I quickly made my way over, trying to avoid eye contact with anyone around me. I took a seat and popped my pen and student ID on the table and shortly after a lady came over to confirm my name and that I was on the law course. After ticking me off her list, she asked if I required any tissues which I found odd, but then noticed her staring at my arm.

In the rush of everything happening, I had not noticed the size of the gash on my arm. It was huge and there was blood covering my entire forearm and the palm of my hand. I had rested it on the desk and now there was a red handprint that looked like something out of a horror movie. Taking her advice, I asked if I could have some wet wipes to clean myself off.

As the lovely lady trundled off to the front of the hall to find me some first aid, I looked myself up and down and realised what a state I was. Not only had I cut my arm, but my t-shirt was ripped, exposing part of my chest and my jeans had a cut along the leg seam. I looked like something out of the Walking Dead. I had essentially burst through the front doors like some mad escapee from a mental institution before declaring to everyone I had arrived while covered in blood.

How the hell I was able to make my way over to my seat without anyone screaming I'll never know.

A short while later, I was given some wipes and I brushed myself off as the head of our course explained the format of the exam. It was two hours long and you were to answer two of the six questions. You could not leave or go to the toilet within the first hour and if you were to need the loo, you had to be accompanied by an invigilator and could not speak.

With all of the good luck pleasantries out of the way, our time started.

I flipped over the page and instantly my heart sank.

On the first page, there was neither of the two topics I had studied. I panicked and looked to the next page where there were two more questions. To my relief, one I could answer but there was still one more I needed and the final question was on the back cover. Holding my breath, I slowly turned the page and let out a massive sigh of relief as I saw it was the second topic I had studied.

I was one lucky guy.

With no time to lose, I began writing ... and writing ... and writing ... Before I knew it, I had filled four pages and had answered the main body of the first question. I took a quick glance up at the clock and worked out I still had an hour and ten minutes left. Knowing time was on my side, I wrote a conclusion to my first question and then started planning my next answer. I looked back up at the clock and could see an hour had gone. Remembering I could now go to the toilet, I sat there debating if I really needed the loo. Was my mind playing tricks on me?

Suddenly, a lad sat next to me stuck his hand up in the air.

I watched as one of the invigilators hurried over to him and he whispered to the invigilator he needed the toilet. Despite not being desperate, I thought I would take the chance to use the facilities too and so whispered to the gentleman that I also needed to use the restroom. Reluctantly, we were both given permission, but it was pointed out that we could not talk to one another under any circumstances and we would be monitored in the toilet to make sure of this. We both agreed and understood the protocol. Despite it seeming over the top, I could understand why it had to be done – no doubt people would exchange notes if they could.

All three of us started off to the toilets and after being told again the circumstances of the situation, we made our way into the gents. Both my toilet break friend and I headed to the two urinals that were available and unzipped. The second I started, I realised just how badly I had needed to go. Knowing it best I made no eye contact at all, I kept facing forwards. With just the sound of the two of us relieving ourselves, I suddenly realised mine sounded much like the urinal was filling up. I looked down and was shocked to see that there was a blockage because of chewing gum and the liquid was about to surge over the bowl.

I looked around in a panic as what to do, the last thing I wanted was to sit through the next hour with piss soaked trainers. With the liquid now at the brim, I freaked and took a big step back and across and joined the guy in the urinal next to me.

Well, you can imagine his shock as I squeezed in next to him and continued pissing away.

I could see he wanted to shout, but with the fear of being disqualified from the exam he just stared at me as if to say, "What the hell are you doing?"

My movement had not just been noticed by my urinal friend but also the invigilator.

"What are you guys doing?" he shouted.

"My urinal filled up so I had to join his," I explained.

"Are you swapping notes?" he snapped.

"Yeah, that's exactly what we are doing. I'm showing him the definition of murder along my shaft," I said sarcastically.

Thankfully, the invigilator laughed and pointed out my penis probably wasn't big enough to fit that all on anyway.

Laughing, I finished up before quickly zipping up and turning to show him I was holding nothing, nor had I anything written on my hands that could have helped either of us to answer the question.

I washed my hands and waited to be escorted back to the hall. The entire time, I could feel laughter building up inside me and a stuttering cough from the invigilator suggested he was struggling to keep in his laughter too.

Feeling pretty uncomfortable, but still laughing to myself about everything that had happened, I made my way back to my seat rather timidly and sat back down. I still had fifty minutes left and with my plan already written down for my second answer, I tried to block out the events of the toilet and set about writing.

Again, I wrote a huge amount and so quickly that my hand actually began to hurt. I rolled my wrist around in a circle and rubbed the joint to try and ease the pain as I forced myself to write down everything I could.

In what felt like the blink of an eye, the fifty minutes were up and an alarm sounded from the front of the hall to signal it was time for everyone to stop writing and put down their pens. I sat back in my chair and stared up at the ceiling, not just relieved to be finished but also to have actually made it to the exam at all *and* have the questions I wanted came up.

It was nothing short of a miracle, in all honesty.

As my paper was collected, I was given permission to leave and you won't be surprised to hear I got out of the hall and was looking for a bus to get home as quickly as possible. I didn't want people staring at me and asking questions about the state I was in. Quite frankly, the whole thing had been an embarrassment. All I wanted was to get back to my flat, have a shower and rest up to be ready for my next exam, which was the next day.

And so that's exactly what I did.

Chapter 13:

The next day, I woke at 07:00. I didn't actually have to be up that early because my exam was not until noon, but I thought waking up early would give me a chance to go through my notes and remind myself of any important information before I took on the paper.

After fixing up a slice of toast topped with some marmite in the kitchen, I made my way back to my room locked my door and shut my window in order to block out any outside noise and allow me to concentrate as much as possible on my notes.

The silence was almost eerie as I sat and stared at the black and white letters covering the A4 sheet of paper in front of me. Is there anything worse than sitting down and reading something over ten times and it not going in at all? Literally just reading the same thing over and over and not being able to remember any of it. It's painful.

But that is exactly what happened and I could feel myself stressing about it.

Trying to take a different approach, I decided to stop reading the notes and to put my mind on something else, then, when I was more relaxed,

I could go back to tackling the notes and hopefully have some better luck.

Going ahead with my idea, I decided to look at ordering some food. I had only had a slice of toast and with my exam being at noon, I needed a sort of brunch to get me through it. I remembered Anna mentioning that there was a café not far from us that delivered and so I decided to go ahead and look them up.

From the images on their website, it looked like your bog-standard greasy café. There was a typical little canopy overhanging the front of the shop with an old-school open sign hanging in the window. I scrolled down to the menu and started to add things to my basket. It was awesome. You could essentially build your own breakfast and choose how many of each things you wanted. You want ten sausages? You can have ten sausages! Obviously, I didn't go that mad but at least I knew I had the option. Instead, I settled on two rashers of bacon, two sausages, a small tub of beans, tomatoes and a couple of hash browns.

Having spent fifteen minutes deciding what to eat and with my order going to be twenty five minutes before it arrived, I went back to my notes and tried reading over them again. My little plan had worked! Suddenly, my mind was switched on and I was able to read a line before covering it, reciting it over out loud and then checking whether I had it correct. I did this a few times before eventually I could do the whole page without even having to read the line beforehand at all.

The little victory filled me with confidence and just as I finished the last line, my phone buzzed next to me.

I picked it up and read a message to say that my delivery driver was outside our halls and could I come to collect my food. Feeling both excited and hungry, I wasted no time in heading downstairs and greeting him at the front door to the halls. As I took the bag from him, I was surprised at just how heavy it was. I know I had ordered a fairly decent amount of food but it felt like a meal for two!

I thanked the driver for the food and felt bad that I had forgotten a tip for him, but he didn't seem fussed. I guess he sort of expected it, especially when delivering to a university – students are hardly rolling in enough money to leave a tip for every delivery they receive.

I rushed upstairs and into the kitchen. It was empty as it had been the last few times I had gone to eat in there. The truth was, everyone was finding the stress of exams hard and they were either at the library sifting through books or in their rooms beavering away at past papers. The last thing you wanted was to be in an environment like a kitchen where people could be clattering pots and pans together or cooking with the absurdly loud extractor fan on.

I grabbed a clean knife and fork from the draining board by the sink and sat down at the table. I fished my hand into the plastic bag I had been given by the driver and pulled out the cardboard box which had my food in.

The sight was disgusting.

As I pulled the box out, grease leaked through the bottom right hand corner. At first I thought the beans may have just spilt, but opening it up I could see that they were securely held in a little plastic box of their own.

I looked at the bacon and sausages inside and could see that they were dripping with fat. I felt like ringing the café up and complaining, but at the end of the day I paid £6.50 for all this food and delivery so I could hardly complain. I decided to fetch a plate and eat off that rather than out of the box itself. If I were to cut anything on the cardboard it would just fall apart because of how wet it was.

I dumped all the contents on to my plate and looked at the slop that presented itself in front of me. I debated whether to just bin it but the truth is I didn't want to waste it and plus it saved me time on cooking something else, which was time I could use for revising instead. I picked up my fork and pierced one of the sausages. I looked it up and down one last time before taking a bite. Chewing on it, I wasn't sure whether it was made out of something that went oink, neigh or woof. Either way, though, it tasted like carpet.

I chewed and chewed until I eventually ground it down to a small enough size to swallow. I actually felt the grease from the sausage line my trachea as it slipped down my throat. Wincing, I picked up another slice and again chewed for what felt like an eternity until I could swallow.

Now, I know what you might be thinking. Why have a big breakfast? Why not eat lunch just before you go in? Well, with a noon start time, I did not want to eat just before the exam and sit there with a full stomach. I knew I would feel bloated and tired – I would often slip into a sort of food coma after eating. To avoid this, I found myself eating a large breakfast. It would give me time to digest it and would provide energy to my body for when the exam started.

After forcing the food down to my stomach, I made my way back to my room and started going over my notes again. After a good session of reading through things and feeling confident again – that I knew all that I needed to – I decided to take a break. It was about thirty minutes before I had to leave and I had heard one of the best things to do before sitting an exam was to take your mind off it.

With this in mind, I decided to stick on something funny on YouTube, just a simple *cats getting scared* video. Well, after watching one, I quickly found myself on the next and soon twenty minutes had passed.

It was as I let out a particularly big laugh that I felt my stomach rumble.

Holding my belly, I thought maybe I had mistaken a sound from the video for my body and so I hit pause. I sat in silence for about twenty seconds and no noise. Smiling to myself at how paranoid I was, I leant forward to hit play again and the second I did, my stomach let out the most almighty rumble. I held my stomach and felt the vibration pass through my hand.

Not now, I thought to myself.

After yesterday's nightmare, the last thing I wanted was another today.

I held on to my stomach as another rumble rang out of it.

The good news was that, although there were rumbles, I did not actually feel unwell. It was just as if my stomach was unsettled, but there was no sign of anything worse.

Relieved but still wary of the noises, I decided to start making my way across campus to the exam hall. I left myself plenty of time compared to yesterday and arrived ten minutes before it was due to start. I made my way inside along with all the other students and took my seat towards the front of the hall.

After the usual routine of being explained the rules of the exam and what we are to do (exactly the same as the day before), we were handed our papers. For some reason, I had totally forgotten about my gamble up until the questions landed on my desk. I had to hope that the two questions I had chosen to revise came up as otherwise I would be screwed.

Flipping open the paper, I was over the moon to see that questions one and two were both exactly what I wanted.

I immediately started to plan each of my answers as I could hear people still rifling through their papers. The noise of paper being flicked and twisted echoed around the room, which I was very thankful for as it covered the noise of my stomach letting out another groan. I carried on scribbling away for about another ten minutes or so when I felt another grumble beginning to rise. However, this was not just a grumble as I felt my stomach tightening. I could tell there was a build-up of gas and truthfully and rather horribly I needed to relieve myself of some trapped wind.

So here's the scenario: I had trapped wind that needed shifting in a room that was large and echoed and was filled with every one of my course mates. Basically, any student's worst nightmare. And now the rustling paper sounds were non-existent as everyone had decided on the questions they were answering.

I was in a real spot of bother.

I carried on writing but the inevitable was going to happen and I needed to find a way of drawing as little attention to it as possible.

I thought to myself about how to tackle it. Paper! At the start of the exam, everyone was making noise with the paper. I knew that me flicking through the paper would not cover the noise, but how about if I "accidentally" dropped my paper on the floor and relieved myself at the same time as the noise of the booklet hitting the floor? It was not a great plan by any means, but it was the best I had.

I started to nudge the booklet to the end of the table with my elbow, using my best acting skills to look as if I could not tell what I was doing. I felt the booklet slip off the end of the table and I looked down to see it falling to the ground.

Now it was all about timing.

The booklet hit the ground completely flat, making a loud slapping noise that echoed across the hall.

Two seconds later, I farted.

Well, you can imagine the embarrassment I felt. Not only had I mistimed my cover up, but in doing so, I had drawn all attention to myself by making the noise with the booklet in the first place and then proceeding to fart. I might as well have announced to the room I was going to fart and then done so, my plan was that much of a cock up.

As you can imagine, there were a lot of sniggers across the hall and the head invigilator told everyone to be quiet and focus on their work. Nonetheless, you could tell from the tone in her voice she found it funny and was trying to hide the laughter that was building up within her. To top it all off, one of the invigilators had actually walked up from behind me and picked up my booklet to hand to me.

Well, thanks a lot, mate, I thought to myself.

Now even people who weren't able to tell where the noise had come from because they were sat further away from me could work out who the culprit was. Why not hang a giant arrow from the ceiling pointing at me just to make it completely clear in case anyone was still in any doubt?

I cursed under my breath as I felt my face becoming redder and redder with embarrassment. To try to cover up the quickly growing colour filling my cheeks, I placed my left hand on my left cheek. Heat filled my hand and I was grateful as I felt my cheek cooling down as a few seconds passed. In those few seconds, I also heard the sniggering die down, although I knew the second everyone was allowed to talk outside I would no doubt be the topic of conversation rather than the paper.

I continued to try to answer the questions but, truth be told, my mind was elsewhere. I could not block out what had just happened and after reading back over a sentence I had just written and seeing it made no sense at all, I realised I had totally lost concentration. The problem was the more I tried not to think about it, the more I did. I know it sounds crazy but let me give you an example. Think of an elephant. Now try to read this sentence without thinking about one. I bet you can't. Even now as you read on, I bet it's swinging its trunk about, isn't it? Well, that's exactly the problem I had.

To try to put myself back on track, I actually decided to put my pen down and just sit back in my chair and watch the clock. I literally did nothing except count the big hand do a full three hundred and sixty degrees five times in a row and thought about football. I know it sounds crazy, but for me, if I am caught in a hard place, I tend to just switch off and think about games I have attended with my dad and friends and think of the good (and bad times) I have witnessed first-hand at Craven Cottage, the home of Fulham FC.

With a clearer head and a more relaxed feeling, I picked up my pen, looked over my plans for the questions one last time and began writing.

It was like the flick of a switch. I went from making no sense at all to a flowing rhythm with all the knowledge I had built up over the year firing out of my fingertips. I wrote so quickly and so efficiently that I actually ended up finishing with ten minutes left. As a result, I had time to go over my answers and correct the spelling mistakes I had made. It was honestly probably one of the best exams I have ever sat, albeit one where I farted so loudly people may have thought I shit myself.

With the alarm sounding to signal the end of the exam, I put my pen down and waited for my paper to be collected and to be told I could leave. Unsurprisingly, I was instantly pointed at by people as I left the hall, but the truth was the fact that everything had gone so well after that little incident I didn't really mind. I was on too much of a high to really care and when I did get asked about the whole thing, I just laughed and said, "Yeah, I would avoid that café around the corner." It paid off making a joke about it too, as people joined in and within seconds the subject had moved on to the paper.

Chatting away to people, it seemed everyone was in a similar boat to me. They were very happy with the paper overall and thought they had smashed it! As cheesy as it may sound, it was actually such a nice feeling walking to the bus stop with others who were as happy as I was with how they had done.

There was not a sad face in sight and there was only one exam to go...

Chapter 14:

After the success of the exam the day before, I was still on a high and knowing that everything would be over after today, well, it just added to my already positive mood. It was morning and my exam was not until the afternoon, but truthfully I was at that stage where I just wanted to finish everything. I would have sat the paper there and then in my room if I had the option to; I was that desperate to have it all done. But I still had about three hours until it started.

Instead, I had to kill some time. Well, you know those videos of cats getting scared that I spoke about earlier? It turns out the ones of *people getting scared* are just as funny and before I knew it, I was chuckling away at a grandma swearing at her grandson after he jumped out in front of her as she left her room. This killed an hour and soon I was thinking maybe it was best I had something to eat. Obviously, I was not going to take anything from the café after the disaster the day before, but I thought a quick bowl of pasta with some tuna would easily tide me over.

Arriving at the kitchen, I could already see that someone was inside and entered to find Layla furiously stirring away at a saucepan on the hob. She was so focused on what she was doing that she didn't even hear me walk in. Her hair was wild and it was clear she was stressed by the way she was mumbling away to herself.

I let out a little cough to let her know I was there and she span round quickly to face me. I was shocked to see her eyes red and filled with tears.

Without hesitation, I walked over to check if she was alright, but before she could answer me she just flung herself into my arms and started to sob. She wrapped her arms around me as I counselled her, telling her everything would be okay, but the truth was I still didn't know what was wrong.

After a while, she pulled herself away and explained it was the stress of the exams that was getting to her. She was just trying to make food, but she said like her revision, it was going wrong.

I told her to take a seat and relax for a bit. I could see that she had attempted to make sausage and mash, however the potatoes had not been cooked long enough and so trying to mash them was near impossible because of how hard they still were. As I was already intending on cooking, I thought I would cook for us both. Unfortunately, the mash was not salvageable and Layla explained she only was having sausages – which she hated – as they were the only thing she had left in her fridge and she had not had time for a shop recently.

I took the sausages out of the pan, popped them into a bowl before placing them on a shelf in the fridge. I then proceeded to go about making my pasta and tuna but for two people instead of one. While doing so, I chatted to Layla about why she was finding it so hard. She was quick to point out the word studying contained the word dying as well. Coincidence? She didn't think so.

She explained it was the pressure of it all that had got to her. She was a bright girl, however, the problem was exam situations proved her downfall. It's similar to any sports people – they could be the best at training and be tipped to win the next tournament, but when it comes to them actually taking it on in front of thousands of people, they crumble.

On a personal note, I have a mixed feeling on exams and also the education system itself. I think for people who thrive in exam situations it is brilliant, but what about those who struggle with them but are incredible at the practical side of things? They may not be the best at getting it down on paper, but presented with it in a real life scenario in front of them they could be the better person for the job. Also, when are schools going to introduce life skills like filling out forms or educating you on the best way to get a mortgage? When I am older and want to buy a house, I want to know how to go about it and I doubt the bank will be impressed if I tell them I have no idea what I am doing but can tell them the area of a circle ...

Anyway, back to the kitchen. I went ahead cooking the food and chatting to Layla, trying to put her in a more positive mood. She asked me to help her with some questions and popped off to get her revision cards. She had made out to me that she had not got a clue, but going through the questions with her, I was astounded at the fact she recited the answer virtually word for word each time. After ten minutes, we stopped and I smiled as I told her how brilliant she was and perhaps she had much more knowledge than she appreciated.

I short while later, I served up the food. It was a very basic tuna and pasta salad with a dollop of mayo mixed in and some peas to add some colour to the dish. It was nothing special but, from the expression on Layla's face, I could see it meant an awful lot to her.

We shovelled the food down us, realising just how hungry we were and before long I picked up two empty bowls to put into the dishwasher. It was just as I closed the door on the dirty dishes I felt an arm come round me as Layla squeezed me tightly. She whispered in my ear thank you before letting go and wishing me all the best for my exam. I thanked her before we both made our way out of the kitchen and to our rooms.

It turns out that the cooking and chat with Layla worked out perfectly timewise for me and I had forty minutes before my exam started. I gathered up my stuff as usual and headed out of the flat to the bus stop around the corner. A short ride over to the other campus for one last time and I was soon stood outside the exam hall with my fellow classmates. We were all eager to get on with it. This was the last one of our first academic year and after it we were free ... well, until next year at least.

Shuffling our way in, I took my seat before readying myself for the questions to be handed to me. Remember, I had still revised way less topics than I should have, but for some reason I felt confident that the ones I had studied would come up just as they had for the previous papers.

And guess what ... they did! You were expecting me to say they didn't, weren't you? Yep, I got *that* lucky again. I think I pretty much smiled the entire way through writing my answers – everyone else there must have thought I had smoked a joint before coming or something.

In truth, it was a pretty uneventful paper. It was not a paper that I thought went amazingly, nor one I thought went really badly; it was probably the most standard paper I had ever answered. It was when the alarm went off to sound the end to it that the realisation really set in.

I was done. Done! No more exams! Freedom!

I walked out of the exam hall filled with joy! Everyone was giving hugs to one another and talking about how happy they were to be finished. Next thing it was time to celebrate!

Now, the thing was, my exams finished way before any of my flat mates. They still had a week to go and it was a day after Freddie's last exam that we were all heading to the end of year summer ball, which we had heard was one of the most epic nights at university.

In the meantime, therefore, the only people who had finished were my course mates. Now, you have probably noticed I have hardly mentioned any of my course mates. It is not that I did not get on with them, far from it, – except for Andy, of course – it was just that I had found such a good relationship with my flatmates that any nights out I would end up spending with them. I would often revise and chat with my course mates, but the idea of a beer together had never come up in conversation really.

That was all about to change, however. In fact, I would not just be celebrating with a few of them; it seemed that virtually everyone was heading down to the SU for a drink. Well, as you are probably already aware, I am always well up for a drink and so did not need asking twice whether I was joining. I almost ran with Tom down to the watering hole where already there was a big queue at the bar. I offered to get Tom and drink and he gladly accepted and while I queued, he popped off to find us a table.

Not too long after, as I was paying, Tom tapped me on the shoulder and explained that there was nowhere we could sit with all tables taken. I was a little gutted but as I turned, I saw two girls sat on a bench. The bench could easily hold six so I said to Tom it would be worth asking them if we could join them. Sure enough, they invited us to sit with them and instead of trying to have two separate conversations, they involved us in theirs by asking who our celebrity crushes were. Well, quite taken back by the forwardness of it all, I decided to ask them theirs first while I thought of one. Jonny Depp and Chris Hemsworth were their two. Tom was next and he decided on Margot Robbie. Now, I am a big fan of Margot Robbie but, as she was now Tom's, I decided on Mila Kunis.

After a little more conversation on why we had chosen them, we introduced ourselves to one another. Olivia and Sarah were the two girls' names and I have to say they were a real breath of fresh air. Easy going and a very good laugh. Not only that, they were outgoing and not afraid to throw some jokey insults around – apparently, I could be used as a mop if was turned upside down my hair was so curly, something I cannot deny, in all honesty.

Time flew by and after having a game of pool together, we were eventually told it was last orders. Although only 23:00, it was a Thursday and we had been told the SU would be closing earlier to avoid people getting too drunk and disturbing people who were trying to sleep and still had exams to take on.

Talking of drunk – I was.

I was at that stage where I was sipping at my beer but not enjoying it, just forcing it down my neck. Eventually, I took the last gulp from my glass and as we were leaving, Olivia and Sarah invited us to go to a club with them. Although the uni was shutting early, there was a club not far from us that stayed open till late. It was about a twenty-minute taxi ride away and, being as tipsy as I was, I agreed on behalf of both myself and Tom that we would join them.

The only problem I had was having filled my bladder with another pint of alcohol, I needed the toilet and couldn't last a whole twenty-minute taxi ride. As I made my excuses to head back inside, the girls said they would wait just outside with Tom.

Unfortunately, as I went to open the front door to the bar, I was met by the landlord who said to me that they were closed and I could not go back inside to use the toilet. I tried to reason with him but he said if he were to do it once, he would have to do it over and over again.

To be honest, I understood his logic and instead he politely pointed out that round the side of the building was a car park with no CCTV, so I could go there and have no problems.

Seeing everything that happened, the others asked what I was up to. I explained the bar was closed but there was an outdoor toilet just around the corner – which was technically true.

Wanting to save on time and knowing that there was no CCTV to see me, I started to unzip my trousers the second I got around the corner. In my drunken state, I was struggling to get the zip undone, but eventually I pulled it open.

It was just as I undid the button on my jeans that my left foot gave from underneath me.

That's not to say I was so drunk I fell over, it's actually because I fell down a hole.

I stuck out a hand and twisted my body to try to break my fall while shouting. I caught my right hand on some jagged stones as I tried to grab anything on the way down. I landed in a crumbled heap at the bottom of this pit and looked up to see the dark sky above me. I must have been about three feet down and looking around me, I realised I was lying on top of some sort of gas works piping. I was scared that I may have burst one of the pipes, but was relieved that I could not smell any gas and there appeared to be no serious damage done.

Knowing I needed to get out, I tried to pull up my arm in order to use it as a means of levering myself out, but it was wedged. I tried my other arm but that was stuck too. I tried to twist my upper body but it was no use. With my arms stuck, I tried moving my legs and to my relief they were free, unfortunately, though, this just meant I could move my legs and my upper body still remained fixed in place. I was aware that the others were probably wondering where I was and it would not be long till they would come and investigate.

With time against me, I slammed each one of my feet into the side of the pit to create a makeshift foothold. Then, taking a deep breath in, I pushed down as hard as I could to try to prise my shoulders and arms out of the position they were stuck in. My hips rose into the air and it looked rather odd with my pelvis so high but my feet and shoulders stuck down low. I felt a little bit of give and I closed my eyes as I pushed even harder. I could feel whatever it was catching my right shoulder giving and I opened my eyes to try to look and see whether I needed to readjust my feet to help free myself.

To my horror, as my eyes opened, I saw three figures stood at the top of the pit staring down at me. It was Tom, Olivia and Sarah. They stood in silence looking down at me. My hips were aloft in the air, my trousers were now round my ankles due to all my shuffling around I had been doing and my face was bright red due to all the effort I had put in.

It was fair to say I looked like a bloody idiot.

"Oh. Hi, guys!" I said in a panic.

"What the hell are you doing down there?" asked Tom.

I explained to them what had happened and after they had stopped laughing and taken a selfie with me – much to my annoyance – they helped me get out. It was not an easy job, either. Tom had to lower himself in and it took at least two minutes of him kicking away at the walls of the hole to free up enough space for me to roll over.

As I eventually hauled myself out of the hole, I realised just what a state my clothes were in. I was covered in dust and rubble from where Tom had kicked away the stones around me and the back of my shirt had some kind of sticky substance that had glued itself to the fabric from where I had been lying on the pipes. I looked an absolute state and it was obvious there was no way I was going to be let into the club we had planned on going to.

Instead of wasting everyone's time, I just headed back to my flat and told the others to have a good night. The walk back felt like an eternity, I was embarrassed and, to be honest, a little worried the selfie they had taken might circulate around group chats and I would end up being the talk of campus, but for all the wrong reasons.

As I got back to my halls, I met Frank outside. Although it was late and I knew he had exams, I was not at all surprised to see that he was smoking away and looked as if he had no intention of going in soon. I stood and had a chat for him for a while and he explained he had already sat one exam and had two left that he was feeling confident about.

I was amazed.

The bloke spent half of his time at university high or planning on getting high, how the hell was he able to take in any information – let alone *enough* information – to be confident about his upcoming exams? To be honest, I did not quite buy his confidence and after a quick chat about how happy I was now that I had finished, I headed up to my room.

I made sure as I entered the flat that I closed the door behind me as quietly as possible. I knew everyone had exams left and the last thing I wanted to do was disturb their sleep. A decent night's sleep can make all the difference between producing a good answer and a bad answer. I inched my way to my room before doing the same with my bedroom door. Inside, I got a look in the mirror and could see my top was ripped on the shoulder where I was feeling the pain. I also noticed a black substance on my back.

I took my top off for a closer look. The most horrible smell that was coming from it and as I sniffed it, I knew that no amount of Fairy Liquid or Ariel was going to get whatever it was out of the cotton. Instead, I just chucked it in the bin before throwing the rest of my clothes into the laundry ready to wash for tomorrow. I then hopped in the shower and cleaned myself off before jumping into bed. I lay there in the dark and could not help myself as I started to smile. I had finished! It was finally sinking in that I had done it. I had risked it but got the result I wanted! On such a high, I found it difficult to get to sleep, but honestly I didn't care – I had nothing to do for the next week expect relax and celebrate.

Chapter 15:

The next day, I woke at 12:30. I actually had to do a double take when I looked at my clock but I had definitely read it correctly. I think the mental strain the exams had put on me and having them in such quick succession meant that my body just took the chance to shut down when it knew everything was over. God knows what would have happened if I had to take another paper! Realising I had nothing to do, I picked up my phone and scrolled through the world of Facebook and Twitter. I also checked the law WhatsApp group I was a part of, which also included Tom, to see if he had posted the selfie from the night before, but I was glad to see it was just full of "We finished!" and "Well done, everyone!" messages.

After killing an hour or so, I went off to make myself some breakfast. It felt rather odd sat in the kitchen watching Frank cook some food for lunch while I sat down with a bowl of cereal, it was as if we were in two different time zones. I was also dressed in my dressing gown while Frank looked more sensible in his jeans and black t-shirt. I munched away and had a chat with Frank, who said he was looking forward to finishing and was envious that I was already done. I had to agree I was happy, but I was gutted that we did not all finish at the same time. Instead, I was stuck for another few days before I could celebrate with all of my closet friends properly.

With nothing to do, I decided to do what any student does when they are bored – I started a new TV series. What TV series, you might be wondering? Well, it was Game of Thrones. I had never seen an episode before but had heard all about it and how amazing it was. My dad had recently purchased Sky, too, which meant that I would be able to watch it on my laptop using his login. Knowing how many episodes there were, I decided to stock up on snacks and drinks so that if I did get into it, I wouldn't have to leave my room.

Six hours later of constant viewing and I think it was fair to say that I was hooked. All the snacks – crisps, chocolate, biscuits and a sandwich – had disappeared. My room looked like a bomb had gone off in the local corner shop there were so many empty wrappers and bags spread about. It was as I sat back on my bed, having ended another episode on a cliff-hanger, that I thought maybe it was time I got some fresh air. I'll admit I still had not got dressed and given it was eight in the evening, maybe it was an idea I did something with what little time I had left in the day.

Feeling like a lazy slob, I got up and had a quick shower. It was while rubbing shampoo in my hair I thought about poor Layla, Anna, Freddie and Frank who had probably either just done another day of hard revision or sat an exam. Knowing what it was like to be in that situation, I took sympathy and decided I was going to help them feel a bit better. I jumped out the shower, got dressed and slipped on a pair of trainers. I then grabbed a shopping bag and headed to the local supermarket, about a five minute run away.

On arrival, I purchased some pizza bases, tomato sauce, cheese, ham and mushrooms. A quick spin on the self-checkout and I was on my way back to my flat.

I went in the kitchen to see if anyone was already cooking, but it was empty. I decided to go and check if everyone was in and started with Layla. She was looking exhausted again and I could tell she was struggling with whatever it was she was studying. In the gentlest voice I could muster, I asked if she was hungry and the reply of "Starving!" was exactly what I was expecting, given how much time was being spent studying instead of eating.

Checking on the others, I discovered they were all in the same boat and so I told everyone to make their way to the kitchen in thirty minutes.

I beavered away in the kitchen and was surprised at how simple it was to make the pizzas. Don't get me wrong, I had cheated and bought the bases pre-made but the rest of it was a piece of cake. With them all prepared together, I took advantage of the many shelves in the ovens we had available to us and stuck all the pizzas in at once. I made sure I kept a close eye on them through the glass door as the last thing I wanted to do was burn the surprise for everyone.

About ten minutes later, I started taking them out, with the top shelf first and working my way down. I then dropped a message into the flat WhatsApp group chat, saying that there was something waiting in the kitchen. I will be honest, the pizzas were by no means gourmet. In fact, they were really nothing special but you would not have believed that from everyone's reactions.

It was amazing to see that such a simple thing meant so much.

Feeling rather chuffed with myself, I sat down with them and dove into the food. It was the first time in what felt like an age that we were all back together talking again and thankfully the topic wasn't revision. Instead, I told the guys about me falling into a hole to give them a laugh and that brought us on to the subject of when Anna's dad drove his car into some roadworks late at night once. Turns out he took out all the cones and had to call the AA to tow him out. It cost him a fortune to pay for all the equipment he broke and his car was a right-off, too! Apparently, he had never admitted to his wife what had happened and claimed the car was stolen and he made a false police report which Anna helped him forge to show her mum!

Looking back, I honestly think it was a night like that everybody needed and I could see just on Layla's face alone how much more relaxed she was to be getting away from the stress of it all. With time flying by, it was not long until the first yawn started and that triggered a chain reaction. As much as I could have stayed up and continued swapping stories, I knew they couldn't and so I volunteered to wash up the plates while they all headed to bed, although Anna insisted on helping me with things before she hit the hay.

With everything clean and ready, I went to bed myself. I knew it was only a few days longer before we could all start celebrating together but it was feeling like the longest few days of my life.

Chapter 16:

Eventually, the day came around where Layla finished her final exam. She was the last one out of all of us, but she was done! We wasted no time in celebrating by actually meeting her outside the exam hall with a can of cold Strongbow Dark Fruit. With no hesitation, she grabbed it from my hand, cracked it open and chugged it all down in the space of about ten seconds. With that kind of buzz already, we knew it was going to be a good night and we headed off to the SU and with the rest of Layla's course mates to begin drinking.

Jägerbombs, tequila, sambuca, cocktails, pitchers and pints. Pretty much you could name it and I guarantee one of us drank it that night. We stupidly came up with a game that involved starting at one end of the bar and working our way to the other end as a team, taking it in turns to have a drink. Some shots I had not even heard of and were not even on the cash register system, which meant we were just getting charged a standard rate for what could have been an expensive drink, but obviously we didn't mind.

It was about halfway along that I began to see we had some people struggling. Layla and Anna were now seriously slurring their words to the point I could barely understand them and Frank had not said anything for about half an hour. Instead, he sat there with his hand over his mouth, letting out little burps that, to be honest, looked like they could escalate to much more at any moment. Freddie and I, on the other hand, felt pretty good, but admittedly that may have been because of the huge portion of spaghetti bolognese we both had before we came out, that was lining our stomachs.

Trying to think of a way to try to sober the others up, Freddie and I suggested a game of pool and three glasses of water for the others. Well, Frank instantly ruled himself out of the pool as he said he was rubbish anyway, but Anna and Layla were up for it. Now, I must stress that I am pretty shocking at pool and it turned out so was Freddie. Partner this with two girls who could hardly stand and we had what can only be described as one of the most excruciatingly long games of pool I have ever seen. Honestly, it must have been five minutes before a ball was even potted and then the wait after that for another was just as long. It got to the point that it was so bad, Freddie and I started to take balls off the table and put them in the pockets without the girls noticing to speed things up.

Twenty-five minutes later – that's right, twenty-five! – We were still playing with just the black left. Unfortunately, it was a lot harder to take the last ball off the table without the others noticing and so I ended up trying to help Freddie by leaving the black as close to the pocket as possible whenever I had a shot. I knew I really had no chance of getting it in, but at least I could just help finish the game.

Finally, I set it up essentially perfectly. The ball was right by the pocket and just required Freddie to tap it in. The only problem was Layla, who was on his team and insisted that they perform what could be the last shot together. This meant that Freddie could hold the cue and make the shot, but Layla would act as the rest for the cue. Yes, it was as mad as it sounds.

Freddie tried to persuade Layla to let him take the shot by himself, but in her intoxicated state, she insisted. She turned her body to face the ball in order to get the best view possible of how to angle her hand. With the rest made, Freddie placed the cue on her hand and started practicing moving the cue back and forth. To his surprise, Layla suddenly dropped the cue but continued facing forward towards the ball.

"You okay, Layla?" he asked.

With no warning, Layla was suddenly sick and projectile vomited across the table. There was such force behind the vomit that it actually hit the black 8 ball and caused it to roll into the pocket.

"Wooo! We win!" said Freddie, trying to make light of the situation.

I didn't know what to say and was totally taken aback by what had just happened. Unfortunately, and unsurprisingly, it had not gone unnoticed to the rest of the bar. In fact, pretty much everyone was staring at the mess left on the pool table. The only good news was that, because it was so busy, no member of staff could see from the bar what had happened. Knowing it wouldn't be long till they started collecting glasses and did see what had happened, I grabbed Layla by the hand and led her out of the front with the others following in behind. Despite being as drunk as she was, Layla knew we had to get a shift on and so she did well in getting into a sort of jog so we could get as far away as quickly as possible.

In an attempt to get out of sight, we took a different route back to our flat than usual. We cut across the road and to a ten-foot, metal gate, which is where I came across anti-climb paint for the first time in my life. Well, it's safe to say it does exactly what it says on the tin.

Essentially, it caused havoc.

I could not get any real grip with my shoes and the only real way of getting up was to heave myself upwards with my arms and use whatever little traction I could find with any other part of my body to help haul my body over the top of the gate.

After a couple of attempts, I eventually pulled myself up and over before I jumped down on the other side with a big grin on my face. I have to say, I was very pleased with myself – particularly at the strength I had suddenly mustered from thin air. That grin was soon wiped from my face, however, as I watched Freddie slide across the handle of the gate and pull it open before stepping across to the side I was now on.

The others laughed as they followed him through.

Laughing at how quickly I had gone from hero to zero made the walk back to our flat pass quickly, despite the extra-long route we had chosen to use to avoid detection. It must have been an extra mile but, to be honest, what is a mile when it might save Layla from having to pay for a new pool table? Besides, it gave us time to admire just what a shot it was to finish the game …

Back at the flat, it was quickly decided we should call it a night. The last thing we wanted to do was to put ourselves in any worse a state.

After all it was the end of year summer ball the next day.

Chapter 17:

The next morning, everyone was buzzing. I had hardly slept all night. The thought of fairground rides, food, drink and music from late afternoon till the early hours of the morning had been running through my mind all night and the excitement was too much.

I had my suit ready and had ironed my shirt – this was a day that would no doubt be in my memories for years so I really wanted to ensure I was looking the best I possibly could for any photos taken.

I went and knocked on Freddie's door. He called me in and I entered to find him trying on his own suit. He looked very dapper in a lovely navy suit, similar to my own. The only difference was he had gone for a dark purple tie and I had decided on a red one.

"What do you think?" he asked, adjusting his tie in the mirror.

"Mate, you look great!"

I smiled. I could see from the look on Freddie's face he was just as keen for the day as I was, which made it all the better. That's the thing about days like that, even if it were to turn into a shambles with rain and the music turning out to be woeful, I would still be with my best mates and they would make it a day to remember!

With Freddie clearly ready to go, I checked on the others. Anna and Layla, naturally like any girls preparing for a night out, were getting ready together. I found them sat opposite one another with a lamp lighting up Layla's face as Anna carefully applied make up to her eyes. Anna had a serious face of concentration and I could see just how much looking their best meant to the girls so decided to leave without distracting them. The last thing I would want to do is cause any problems before we got going.

The last person to check on was Frank.

I made my way to his room and could hear the sound of rock music through his door. I knocked loudly and he beckoned me in.

I couldn't quite believe what I saw.

There, stood in front of me, was Frank, but not like I had ever seen him before. He looked totally different. His hair had gone from covering his face to being slicked back and perfectly styled and he was wearing a black suit with a maroon tie. He oozed swagger.

I stood there, lost for words. I opened my mouth to compliment him but just mumbled something totally inaudible.

He looked at my face and laughed. "I know," he chuckled. "I decided to make an effort for once."

I smiled.

What I liked most about it all was, despite the new look, he still had that edgy element about him. His silver chain was still there and hanging from his trousers, but with the hair out of his face you could finally get a sense of what he really looked like!

It was clear he was ready and so I said I would quickly get ready myself and hurry the others up as I didn't want to leave him waiting by himself. He thanked me, but said there was no rush as he was happy to keep himself entertained listening to some more heavy rock.

I made my way back to my room and had a shower. Drying myself off, I used a comb and hairdryer for the first time in ages to get my hair exactly as I wanted it – I even applied a little bit of wax! With my hair ready to go, I carefully put on my suit, making sure I kept it as crease free as possible. I slipped on my shoes and adjusted my tie as the final preparation in my bedroom mirror before giving my reflection a nod.

It was time to celebrate the end of first year in style.

Knowing the girls would still not quite be ready, I went and found Frank and Freddie, who were already in the kitchen having a beer each. I grabbed one myself and we raised our glasses to one another. We sat there discussing the various things we expected from the night before we heard the kitchen door swing open.

There, stood in the doorway, was Anna wearing a beautiful, figure hugging purple dress. Her hair was curled and lay across her shoulders and the light colour of her eye shadow brought out her eyes perfectly.

"You look absolutely stunning, Anna," said Freddie, breaking the silence.

"Amazing," Frank and I agreed.

"Thank you, guys, but the real star of the show is here," said Anna, gesturing around the corner.

Layla stepped forward into the doorway and I can say for the first time in my life my breath was taken away.

She was wearing a long red dress that was off the shoulder one side and reached just short of the floor. Her hair was tied up and curled and lying across her naked shoulder.

"Layla, I don't think there's a way to describe just how beautiful you look," I said before I could stop myself.

Layla smiled, blushing and looking at the floor.

I could feel myself going red too as I sat there, unable to keep my eyes off her.

"You boys all look very handsome too, by the way. I reckon we will be the best looking flat out there tonight," said Anna, winking at us all. "Enough chat, anyway. Let's all have a drink before we get going."

We knew drinks were going to be expensive once we got to the event so it was best we had a few before leaving to make sure we didn't spent the rest of our student loan in one hit!

We sat round the table in a rather odd scene.

All of us were dressed up looking as if we should be sipping champagne from a flume and calling one another Claud and Eliza but, instead, we were playing the ring of fire drinking game and forcing each other to down shots of tequila and chug down bottles of beer while singing indie classics.

But the truth is, I wouldn't have changed it for the world.

We drank to the point of being tipsy, but all agreed we needed to keep drink to a reasonable level – as much as we wanted to celebrate, we all wanted to remember the night too!

The clock struck 18:00 and we decided it was probably best we got going soon. We wanted to beat the rush of the crowd and ensure we had a good spot by the stage for whoever it was that was headlining the evening. We decided to give ourselves twenty minutes before leaving, giving us time to gather up anything else we needed or last minute preparations. The girls decided to use the time to top up their makeup while the lads and I decided on a quick beer and chat.

With the kitchen to ourselves, we got talking about the girls.

We all agreed at just how stunning they looked and how any guy would be lucky to have them. To my surprise, Freddie and Frank began really quizzing me on whether anything had happened between Layla and I. Naturally, I told the truth and explained nothing had happened between us, but the lads wouldn't believe me. They began asking lots of questions like whether there had ever been any sign of anything happening, but before we could really get into the meat of the conversation, the girls were back.

"Right then, let's go bring some life to this party!" Freddie shouted.

We all cheered and made our way out of the kitchen and down the stairs to the main entrance. We swung a right around our building, as we always did, to the bus stop. It was heaving with people, all dressed up similarly to us. We squeezed our way into the crowd and as close to the front of the stop as possible. With such a cramped area, I was expecting a bit of trouble and agitation, but with exams finished and the accompanying relief that came with having them out of the way, everyone was just smiling and pleasant to one another.

With the university knowing just how big a day this was and that thousands of tickets had been sold, they had sensibly put on a service of buses, which meant one arrived virtually every two minutes. We ended up hopping onto the fourth bus that came along and were even blessed with having four seats. I volunteered to stand, but everyone insisted they could squeeze me in and so I ended up sitting between Layla and Frank. I looked at Freddie and Anna sat opposite me and Freddie nodded towards Layla with a smile on my face.

I mouthed "no" to him still insisting that there was nothing between us.

It was a fifteen-minute journey to the venue, which was a grand house with acres and acres of land surrounding it. The event itself was in the grounds rather than the house – I mean, it would be insane to let thousands of twenty–twenty-five-year olds-loose in an old Victorian house expecting no damage to be caused.

We hopped off the bus and joined the queue to get in.

A quick scan of our tickets and a short walk into the centre of the grounds meant we could really get a sense of the place. To the left of us was the main stage, which had a long bar running alongside it. Then, to the right, there was an array of food and drink stalls as well as fairground rides.

I pointed to the bumper carts. The others didn't need asking twice, we practically sprinted over to them and arrived just as the previous peoples' ride was ending. Freddie and I teamed up together as did Anna and Layla while Frank decided to jump in with a random person.

"You drive," instructed Freddie.

I leapt into the driver's seat and Freddie dove into the passenger's side.

"Okay, one aim here ... cause chaos!" Freddie smirked at me.

I nodded in agreement.

"Three, two, one!" shouted the man on the tannoy.

I slammed my foot on the accelerator and we immediately surged forward. It had been so long since I had been on this kind of ride that I forgot the speed you can pick up. We raced around the outside before Freddie pointed at a target.

Two very small girls were in a car on the other side of the ride.

"They'll go flying if we hit them," Freddie said, eyeing up our objective.

I flicked the wheel round, performing a quick U turn. I dodged a couple of people heading the other way to us before lining up the girls. I sat myself back as did Freddie, bracing ourselves for impact. The girls were too busy looking around to see us coming. We slammed into them head on at maximum speed. Freddie and I were flung forward – thankfully, we had our seatbelts on, which stopped us from getting any serious injuries. Unfortunately, the girl driving the other car hadn't remembered to wear hers. Her whole body flung forward and she headbutted the steering wheel before bouncing back into her seat.

I sat there in horror as we saw blood dripping from the girl's nose. Her friend quickly leant across and began pinching her nostrils as the wounded girl leant down and produced a tissue from her bag to stop any blood getting on her clothes.

"Oh, sweet God, we've just ruined her day," I whispered to Freddie.

"We? Nah, mate, you were driving, that was all you," he protested.

"Oh, come on," I moaned. "That's not fair!"

Freddie just shrugged.

We got out and made our way over to the girl. I was expecting the worse – for her to slap me or at least scream at me. Instead, as we asked if she was okay, she just laughed and nodded. She held out her free hand and I gladly helped her out, relieved at the fact she was okay with the whole situation. I apologised profusely, but the girl simply held up a hand. I helped her to the side of the ride and down the steps on to the grass. Again, I apologised and, again, she smiled and lifted up her hand for me to stop. I smiled and was just about to offer to buy her a drink, but out of nowhere an evil smirk appeared across her face and she kicked me hard between my legs.

My knees buckled and I wailed at the pain.

"Now we're even," she hissed at me as I grasped my testicles, trying to soothe the agony.

It was torture and I could feel my eyes beginning to fill with water. I breathed sharply in and out, trying to take my mind off the pain and calm my body's reaction.

I felt a pat on my back and looked up through blurred vision to see Freddie stood next to me. "She must have literally just started that time of the month, mate," he said.

I could see he was holding himself back from sniggering and I laughed at his poor attempt at hiding it. The laughter helped take my mind off most of the pain and I sat myself down on one of the steps to get in a more comfortable position.

Freddie sat next to me and I gave myself five minutes to just make sure all the pain had subsided. I was quite lucky in the fact that nobody had really seen what had happened – not even Anna or Layla – saving me from too much embarrassment. I was still quite shocked at how the girl's mood had changed so quickly, though. From an innocent, forgiving angel, she had turned into a ball-bashing nutter.

I stood up and shook my leg about once more, just to make sure I was fully okay. I was still tender but thought alcohol would help subdue the small amount of pain left and so nodded at Freddie and pointed at the closest bar.

We walked over and whilst queuing, could see Anna and Layla off to the side talking to two guys, both of whom were tall, dark and so muscular you could see it through their tight-fitting shirts.

Looking over, I made eye contact with Layla before quickly turning my head away out of embarrassment – she might think I was staring.

I turned to Freddie to ask what he wanted to drink, but before I could ask he gave me a smirk as if he knew something I didn't.

"What?" I asked.

"Luke, you are either stupid or blind or both."

"What do you mean?"

"Wow," he said, rolling his eyes. "It doesn't matter, let's just get these drinks in and grab the girls before those guys get too friendly with them. It would be nice if we all stuck together."

With drinks in hand, we made our way over to the girls. As we approached, the two guys looked us up and down.

"Can we help you couple of pussies?" asked the first one.

"Why would these gorgeous girls want anything to do with you, you little virgin!" interjected the other.

"Actually, you're wrong, I was a virgin until last night," I grinned sarcastically.

"As if!"

"No, I swear, ask your sister."

"Good one. But I don't have a sister"

"But you will in nine months," I quipped back.

Anna and Layla burst out laughing.

Both of the meatheads' faces dropped.

"Whatever. Probably got a dick like a tic tac anyway," they snapped back.

"That explains why your mum's breath is so fresh then," laughed Freddie.

The laughter grew even louder from the girls and, knowing they were beaten, the lads took themselves and their dented egos off into the night, grumbling as they went.

With a new sense of confidence, I offered out my hand to Layla and gestured towards the main stage. She smiled, took hold of it and we made our way over towards the assembling crowd with Freddie and Anna close behind us.

We gently squeezed through the people all huddling at the stage until we found ourselves about five metres from the stage.

"Oh my God," Anna said, pointing in front of us.

There, leaning against the fence, was Frank and he was kissing a girl!

"Yes, Frank!" we all shouted.

Frank, shocked by the noise suddenly coming from behind him, unlocked lips from his new companion and looked around, laughing and giving us a thumbs up. He had lipstick all over his mouth making him look like the joker from Batman, but I could see he didn't care one bit.

He spoke briefly to the girl before both of them came to join us in our little group.

Freddie and I gave him a high five as he introduced Emily to us. "You guys ready?" he asked excitedly.

"You bet!" I shouted.

The special guest had been kept under wraps the whole time – all it said on the ticket purchase was the headliner was a BRIT Award winner and had sold millions of singles. We started guessing who it could be when suddenly all the lights on the stage lit up and smoke began to pour in from each side.

The tension grew as silhouette appeared through smoke.

"London, are you ready?" shouted the figure.

We all screamed and yelled to let him know we were more than ready.

"Then let's party!" the voice shouted again.

The music started and I instantly recognised the tune.

Tinie Tempah came running out of the fog and began rapping. The crowd went wild.

I have been a fan of Tinie Tempah for as long as I can remember and was loving every moment. Song after song I rapped along to and the others were surprised at just how well I knew the lyrics. After an hour-long set, he made his way backstage to the noise of us all cheering his name, "Tinie, Tinie!" It was one of the best performances I had ever seen.

I turned to the others who, like me, were wearing big smiles across their faces.

From nowhere, Freddie grabbed my arm.

"Mate, this is the moment to do it!" he whispered in my ear.

"Mate, nothing has happened between us and I don't have the confidence to do anything about it," I moaned, knowing he was referring to Layla again.

"Has she not said anything to you when you are alone to hint she fancies you at all?"

I wracked my brain. "Well, this one time we were alone and I was in my boxers she complimented my body, and a couple of times she has grabbed my hand."

"Okay, thank God you were not Adam and Eve as there would be no humans on this planet! Wake up and smell the Sambuca, man!"

"Mate, I can't! She's so far out of my league. I just … I just can't"

"Listen to me. How long did you believe in Santa?"

"Ermm, nine years, I guess?" I said, confused at the question.

"If you can believe in Santa for nine years, you can believe in yourself for thirty seconds."

It was the most peculiar way I had ever been given a boost of confidence, but it worked.

I smiled and Freddie could see that his little pet talk, accompanied by the alcohol in my system, had given me the buzz I needed to take things into my own hands. I turned away from him to find Layla, but she was nowhere to be seen.

I asked Anna where she had gone and she explained she had popped off to the toilet.

Freddie urged me to go find her.

Like a passenger running late for their train, I weaved my way in and out of the dispersing crowd and towards the giant toilet sign, which hung high on scaffolding poles above the hordes of people below.

Through a small gap in the crowd, I spotted Layla stood outside the toilets talking to someone, but I couldn't make out who. I pushed round the last couple of people and got a clear sight.

My heart sunk.

There was Layla stood talking to a guy who had his hands on her waist. It seemed like quite a serious conversation between the two and an intimate moment. I froze at the sight and stood there for a few more seconds, watching as the guy took his hands off her waist before gesturing up and down her body and clearly complimenting her.

Although I couldn't hear what was being said, I saw Layla dip her head and laugh.

I was gutted. I had left it too late. I didn't even know whether she would have said yes to me asking her out, but it was the fact that I hadn't even got the chance to ask. I would never know. I had wasted my chance. Idiot.

I turned away and took in a deep breath, trying to compose myself. It felt odd; I had not been in a relationship with Layla – I hadn't even kissed the girl – yet it still felt like a break up of some kind. I started to trudge my way back in the direction of the others, thinking of how I could break the news to Freddie. I guessed I would just have to tell them what happened.

Ahead of me, the crowd had virtually disappeared and I could make out the figures of Freddie, Anna, Frank and his new friend Emily in the distance. I felt something hit my foot and looked down to see a glass bottle by it. It suddenly dawned on me the mess that had been made – cups, wrappers and bottles lay all over the floor. I pulled back my leg to take my still present frustration out on the bottle with my foot when suddenly I felt a hand on my shoulder.

I span around, expecting to see a security guard and receive a telling off, but instead there was Layla.

Without saying anything, she pulled me in close with her hands on my hips and kissed me.

At first, I didn't kiss back due to the shock of what was happening.

After a few seconds, she pulled away and smiled lovingly into my eyes. I smiled back and heard a cheer over her shoulder. I peered around to see the guy she had been speaking to by the toilets pumping his fist into the air.

The confusion on my face must have been evident.

"That's Toby from my course," said Layla.

"But … I … You guys were …" I stuttered.

"He was showing me how to go about finally making my move – he's gay," laughed Layla.

I laughed out of embarrassment at misunderstanding the whole situation. I looked back at her beautiful face before leaning in for a kiss myself.

Holding hands like a couple of newlyweds, we made our way over to Anna and Freddie who, similarly to Toby, were cheering. We got hugs from them both like the happy parents of a bride.

"Finally!" they both sighed. "We thought it was going to take one of you to be on your deathbed before the other told them how they felt!"

I looked around and realised we were now the only people left at the event other than a couple of cleaners who had started picking up the endless amounts of litter that was scattered along the ground. Freddie explained that Frank and Emily had gone ahead to catch an earlier bus and, with little else to do, we all agreed it was best we started heading back to where the buses had dropped us off.

Both the girls had to take off their heels because of the pain they now had in their feet. Fearing they may cut themselves on something on the floor, Freddie and I offered to give them piggybacks to the bus stop.

It was a lot further than we thought and we kept on having to take breaks, struggling to keep the girls on our backs as we ambled our way along the grass.

About ten minutes later, we arrived and to our horror there were no buses.

"Damn it!" Freddie cursed. "This is why Frank and Emily left earlier, they wanted to get back to grab something from Frank's before heading out."

Probably a joint, I thought to myself.

With nobody around and no taxis available either, we decided to walk. There was no more fear of glass and so the girls held onto their shoes and we started to walk along the pavement.

We chatted about the night and looked back on what the year had brought us and before long we were halfway to our halls. We were walking along a long, straight road and it was now dark, with the only source of light coming from the street lamps or the occasional passing car.

The night was quiet and our voices filled the night air, but as we approached the end of a road we could hear whispers and giggling coming from a house on the corner. The four of us crept silently forward, expecting to find a couple of teenagers up late and messing about but, to our surprise, it was Frank and Emily.

"What the hell are you guys doing here?" I whispered to them.

They both jumped at my voice and the rest of us sniggered at their reaction.

I looked around the front garden they were stood in. It was beautifully kept, with a lovely fountain feature in the middle and rows of flowers either side. However, on the main lawn where Frank and Emily were stood, there were endless amounts of pink objects. I pointed at one and asked what the hell they were, unable to make it out the funny shape.

Frank explained that they were the flamingos he had been collecting over the year from the old lady's house! He was now back at the house and had decided to return all twenty-seven he had taken throughout the year. There was literally a flock of them covering the lawn, all in funny positions – some popping their heads out of the hedges and others with gnomes riding their backs.

It was difficult to see the arrangement in all its glory so I took my phone out to use as a torch but before I could, Frank walked up to the door and waved his arms about. A security light burst into life and lit the scene up in all its glory.

We all burst out laughing at the sight – Freddie actually fell on his back he was laughing so hard!

Suddenly, a bedroom light switched on and the curtains flew open.

We all froze as the old lady creaked open her window. She leant out and looked below at the chaos that lay before her eyes.

"Wait there," she said sternly.

We all stood there, unsure what to do. I wanted to run but the truth was this lady was clearly old and if she wanted to tell us off and make us clean it up I would have done so as perhaps the fun had gone a little too far.

A short while later, the door swung open and, dressed in her pink dressing gown and matching slippers, the lady stepped out.

We all immediately began apologising and said we would clean it up and meant no harm.

She held out a hand to stop us speaking.

Like naughty school kids, we stood in a line as she looked around the garden.

"Do you know how many times my daughter has replaced these flamingos?" asked the woman.

"Twenty-seven?" Frank said bluntly.

Layla nudged him in the ribs for his cheekiness.

"Yes," replied the woman. "And I have never had the courage to tell my daughter just how much I hate them. So pick up the fuckers and put them on Beatrice's lawn – house number forty. She won't mind – she's blind!"

So there it is, my first year at university. An eventful one, to say the least. From the lows of flushing a dead grandmother down the toilet, to the highs of landing the girl of my dreams. It is a time I will never forget. I made some fantastic memories, ran up some fantastic debts but, more importantly, met some great people and made some brilliant friends. And you have to remember this was all in year one; there was still another two years to come...

Printed in Poland
by Amazon Fulfillment
Poland Sp. z o.o., Wrocław